SARAH WEEKS

As Simple as It Seems

LAURA GERINGER BOOKS
An Imprint of HarperCollins*Publishers*

Laura Geringer Books is an imprint of HarperCollins Publishers.

As Simple as It Seems
Copyright © 2010 by Sarah Weeks

Library of Congress Cataloging-in-Publication Data
Weeks, Sarah.
   As simple as it seems / by Sarah Weeks. — 1st ed.
      p.   cm.
   Summary: Eleven-year-old Verbena Colter gets through a difficult
summer of turbulent emotions and the revelation of a disturbing family
secret with an odd new friend who believes she is the ghost of a girl who
drowned many years before.
   ISBN 978-0-06-084663-3 (trade bdg.)
   ISBN 978-0-06- 084664-0 (lib. bdg.)
   [1. Adolescence—Fiction.   2. Friendship—Fiction.   3. Family
life—New York (State)—Fiction.   4. Ghosts—Fiction.   5. Identity—
Fiction.   6. Adoption—Fiction.   7. Catskill Mountains Region
(N.Y.)—Fiction.]   I. Title.
PZ7.W42235As   2010   2009025441
[Fic]—dc22   CIP
                                                                AC

10 11 12 13 14   CG/RRDB   10 9 8 7 6 5 4 3 2

First Edition

For Jim, the answer to my prayers.
With love,
SW

CONTENTS

(Author's Note: The chapter headings are all names of actual polkas
and waltzes that could have been played by the Clydesdale Band.)

As Simple
as It Seems

CHAPTER ONE

Top of the Hill

My grandpa Colty died on the same day I was born. Some people believe that when you die, your soul rises out of your body like a mist and goes looking for a new person to live in. If that's true, I like to think that when Grandpa Colty died, he told his soul to come looking for me.

I was born December 21, 1989, at Mount Sinai hospital in New York City. It says so on my birth certificate, which hangs in a fancy gold frame on the wall of my bedroom. It also says that my full name is Verbena Ellen Colter, that my parents' names are Tom and Ellen Colter, and that I weighed four pounds seven ounces when I was born, which is pretty small for a baby in case you didn't know.

It was my mother's idea to name me Verbena. Her maiden name was Wojcik. Her father, a baker, and her mother, a schoolteacher, were both of Polish descent and my mother grew up listening to Polish folk music at home. I was named after one of her favorite songs, a polka called "Verbena, Be Mine."

Our house stands high on the top of a hill, and out in the middle of the yard is a large speckled rock. You can stand on that rock and see all the way down into town. Not that there's much to see. Downtown Clydesdale is made up of four things: the post office, the church, the firehouse, and the bandstand, where rain or shine the Clydesdale Band shows up to play polkas and waltzes on Wednesday nights during July and August when the summer people are around.

When I was old enough to wonder why I had been born in New York City, instead of at Townsend, the big grubby municipal hospital off Route 17 where everybody else I knew had come into the world, I asked my mother about it.

"Sometimes babies get their own ideas about when and where they want to be born," she told me.

For a while I was satisfied with that answer, but eventually I felt a need to ask more questions, and that's how I found out that the reason my mother was in New York City when I was born was because she and my father had gone there to look for my uncle Mike.

Uncle Mike grew up in Clydesdale, but unlike my father he was not a very popular guy. As a kid he bullied his classmates and teased small animals, and when he got older, rumor has it, he did things that were far worse. Nobody much liked him and apparently the feeling was mutual, because the day he turned eighteen, he took off in the middle of the night and never came back. Even though that was years ago, people in Clydesdale still talk about him sometimes.

"Mike Colter was bad news."

"Trouble from the get-go."

"Warped." That's what Francine the postmistress called him once, and she said it right in front of my father too. And even though it was his own brother she was talking about, he didn't disagree with her.

My grandpa's name was Kurt Colter but he went by the nickname Colty. Everybody loved him, and I heard plenty of people say that my father was a chip off the old block. Uncle Mike was a different story.

"Why did you and Daddy go to New York looking for him anyway?" I remember asking my mother.

"Your grandpa was dying, and he wanted to see his youngest son one last time before he passed."

"Did you find him?"

"No," she said. "We didn't. But at least we didn't

come home empty-handed. You arrived a little earlier than expected, but we couldn't have been happier to see you."

Looking back on it now, I guess there were some things I should have noticed. Like the way my parents always looked at each other whenever Uncle Mike's name came up.

Clydesdale doesn't have a grocery store or a gas station or a school of its own. For those things we have to go to Washerville, a slightly larger town, the next one over from ours. On the day of my fifth-grade graduation, I remember standing in the Washerville Elementary School auditorium in a pair of black patent leather shoes a size too small waiting for my name to be called. I was in a terrible mood, but that was nothing new—I'd been in a bad mood since December, when I'd accidentally uncovered a secret my parents had been keeping from me. That secret caused my whole world to shift, like a sheet of tracing paper that no longer matched up with the drawing underneath it.

The graduation ceremony wasn't nearly as big a deal as the ones they had each year for the seniors when they finished high school, but because we would be moving out of the elementary school into the building that housed the upper grades, it was a big enough deal that we got diplomas with our names written on them. Afterward there would be free pizza and Coke at Magaly's, the only restaurant in town.

It was a big day. But it had not started off well.

"I thought you got rid of that," I said, cringing at the sight of my mother in the outfit she'd chosen to wear to the ceremony.

"I love this dress," she said, laying a plump hand over her heart. "It brings back such happy memories. Do you remember that rhyme we made up together when you were a little girl?"

I remembered. *I love you, you love me, Mama and her Sugarpea.* She'd ordered the white dress with peapods printed all over it from a catalog years ago along with a miniature version for me. Matching mother/daughter dresses. At the time I'd been thrilled, but things were different now.

"Can you please wear something else?" I begged.

I had outgrown my peapod dress years earlier, tossing it into a pile of castoffs for the thrift shop. My mother had outgrown her dress as well, but she'd solved the problem by opening the side seams and adding two large triangular panels of white fabric.

"Do you mean it?" she asked, looking hurt. "Do

you really want me to change?"

I nodded.

"I suppose I could wear my blue floral print instead," she said, smoothing the front of the peapod dress with an open palm.

But my father appeared on the stairs behind us, jingling his car keys.

"All set, ladies?" he asked cheerfully. "We'd better get a move on if we want to get good seats."

My dad was fifty-nine years old when I was born, which meant he was seventy the day I graduated from the fifth grade—twenty years older than my mother, and much older than the fathers of the other kids in my class. It was not uncommon for people who didn't know our family to assume when they saw us together that I was his granddaughter. The Colters came from German stock. My father, square jawed and lanky, was the spitting image of Grandpa Colty, and although I bore no resemblance to either one of them, Dad and I both had double-jointed thumbs, which I was told had been a Colter family trait for generations.

My father owned a business called Colter Trim and Mow and oversaw a crew of men who worked for him mowing lawns in the summer and plowing driveways in the winter. He wasn't around much during the day, and by the time he came home at night, he was usually so tired that he would just eat dinner and then turn on the evening news and fall asleep on the couch in front of the TV. My mother did volunteer work, but mostly she stayed at home and doted on me. I was her pride and joy, her Sugarpea, the most perfect little girl in the whole world, according to her. But when I started school and had difficulty learning to read, I began to suspect that my mother's definition of "perfect" was different from the rest of the world's.

It seemed almost magical to me, the way other kids could look at a book and make sense of all those letters. Words were a jumble of meaningless shapes to me. In fact, the only way I could tell if I was holding a book right side up or not was to look at the pictures. I told my mother that I thought there must be something wrong with my brain, and she said nonsense, I probably just needed glasses. As it turned out she was right—I did need glasses—but after I got them I still couldn't read.

Some kids in my class went to the resource room for extra help, but I got my help at home. My mother bought all kinds of games with letter cubes and flash cards, and she worked with me every day after school for months until finally one day it clicked in and I could read.

"I told you there was nothing wrong with your brain," she said. "It's perfect, just like the rest of you, Sugarpea."

Although I learned to read, I never became what you could call a strong reader. At best I was adequate, and in the years to come I struggled with most of my other subjects in school too, including gym because of my small size and lack of coordination. It was obvious I was far from perfect, but because my mother was able to overlook my shortcomings, for the most part I did too, until I hit fifth grade.

That year, things began to change. I had never been particularly moody before, but all of a sudden I was the biggest grouch in the world. I lost my temper at the drop of a hat, especially with my mother, and some-times I would just start crying, for no good reason at all. I felt mixed up and mean. Nothing about me was normal. I had the heaviest mother and the oldest father of anyone I knew. I'd always been small for my age, but unlike the other girls in my class who had shot up and filled out, I stayed just as scrawny as ever. My glasses magnified my eyes and made me look like a bug, and my pale skin and white-blond hair made it appear as if

I didn't have any eyebrows or eyelashes. And then there was my name.

"Verbena Ellen Colter," announced Principal Bartlett from the podium on graduation day.

As I started across the auditorium stage in my miserable little black shoes, my father clapped while my mother leaned heavily on his shoulder in order to climb up onto her chair to take a flash photograph over the heads of the other parents in the audience. I took my diploma, shook the principal's hand, then walked gingerly to the other side of the stage to stand in my designated spot beside Chris Cartwright, who came right before me on the class list. On Chris's other side stood his good buddy, Kevin Brennan.

"Check out Jumbo McDumbo," I heard Kevin whisper to Chris. "I feel sorry for that chair, don't you?"

As the two of them snickered, I turned to see who they were talking about, but of course I already knew. There was my mother climbing down from the chair in her giant peapod dress. Her round face was flushed, and her arms jiggled like pale Jell-O, the elbows hidden in doughy folds of pink flesh. When she caught sight of me looking in her direction, she waved and lost her balance, toppling into the lap of the man sitting next to her. Kevin and Chris fought hard to control their laughter while I stood mortified.

I could have told those boys to knock it off, or at least given them a dirty look—especially Chris, whose guts I already hated for another reason.

But instead of defending my mother, I closed my eyes and wished with all my might that I could be somebody else—anybody besides me.

It was not the first time I had made that wish. Life had seemed so simple the year before. I'd liked school, I was happy at home, and I'd had a best friend named Annie Bingham. It hadn't occurred to me to wonder if I was living a lie or if there was a ticking time bomb hidden inside me getting ready to explode. But by the time fifth-grade graduation rolled around, I had learned that things are not always as simple as they seem.

CHAPTER TWO

Sweet Little Girl

Lots of people are adopted—I know it's not that big a deal. My birth certificate said that Tom and Ellen Colter were my biological parents, and even though I didn't look like either one of them, I had no reason to suspect that it wasn't true. There's a good chance I would have spent my whole life in the dark if I hadn't found the square red envelope addressed to Grace Kincaid tucked into the pocket of my mother's wool coat one afternoon about a week before my eleventh birthday.

"Who's Grace Kincaid?" I asked, holding the envelope out to my mother.

She was standing in the kitchen slicing apples for a pie, a mound of curled green peelings tangled like snakes on the counter beside her. When she saw what I was holding, she turned white as a sheet.

"Where did you get that?" she asked.

"It was sticking out of your coat pocket. I saw it when I went to hang my jacket up in the closet. I thought maybe it was a Christmas card you forgot to mail. So who's Grace Kincaid?"

My mother put down the apple she was holding, reached out, and took the envelope from me. Her fingers brushed against my palm and I noticed they were ice-cold. Without looking at it, she slipped the red envelope into the pocket of her apron. Then she picked up the apple again and with a paring knife began cutting the pale flesh into moon-shaped slivers.

"I've been thinking about your birthday cake," she said. "Which do you think would go better with red velvet—buttercream frosting or cream cheese?"

She could have told me that Grace Kincaid was an old friend from high school, or one of my father's summer customers she'd gotten friendly enough with to exchange Christmas cards. I wouldn't have thought twice about it. But it was clear from the way she was acting that my mother was trying to hide something.

"Who's Grace Kincaid, Mom?" I asked again.

Instead of answering, she covered her face with her hands and burst into tears.

* * *

Half an hour later, I found myself sitting on the living room couch wedged between my parents, fidgeting and feeling nervous as a cat. Even though it was the middle of the day, my mother had called my father at work and told him to come home, something she'd never done before. I knew whatever it was I'd stumbled upon was big.

"Are you sure about this, Ellen?" my father said. "Once it's done, it's done—there won't be any turning back."

"She has a right to know," my mother told him. Then she reached into her pocket and pulled out the red envelope. "Open it," she said, handing it to me.

I slipped my finger under the flap and tore the envelope open. Inside was one of my mother's homemade Christmas cards with a drawing of a sprig of holly on the front. "Happy Holly-days!" it said. When I opened the card, a photograph fell out. It was a picture of me, standing on the front steps of our house with my yellow-and-black plaid book bag slung over my shoulder. My mother had taken it back in September, on the morning of my first day of fifth grade. On the back she'd written "Verbena, age 10."

"Okay," I said. "But I still don't know who Grace Kincaid is."

"She's your uncle Mike's wife," my mother told me.

"I send her a picture of you every Christmas."

I was surprised to hear that Uncle Mike was married, but it wasn't exactly earth-shattering news. I didn't mind if my mother wanted to send them pictures of me. They were family, after all.

Maybe somebody else would have put two and two together and realized that something was up, but I had to have it spelled out for me. The first part of the story my parents told me that day was something I had heard many times before. When Grandpa Colty made his dying wish to see his son, my parents drove to New York City to find Uncle Mike. That story had always ended with Uncle Mike not being found, Grandpa Colty dying, and me getting born, all on the same day. But there was more to the story than that.

My parents followed a lead they'd gotten on an address where someone thought Mike Colter might have lived at one time. The apartment was on the west side of Manhattan, the basement of a brownstone with a wrought-iron gate and three steps down to the door.

"We rang the bell, but there was no answer," my mother said.

Just as they were getting ready to leave, my father thought he heard someone moving behind the door.

Finally it opened and there was Grace.

"She was in a bad way. Soaking wet and shaking like a leaf."

"Was she sick?" I asked.

"No," my mother said. "She was in labor. It had started in the middle of the night, and by the time we got there she was nearly out of her mind from the pain."

"Why didn't she go to the hospital like you did?" I asked. "And where was Uncle Mike?"

"Let your mother finish, Bena," my father said.

My parents went inside and helped Grace to lie down. Then my father said he would call for an ambulance, but Grace got upset. She didn't want him to do that, she said she had no way to pay for it, and besides, she had already made up her mind.

"About what?" I asked.

An uneasy look passed between my parents.

"Grace was an alcoholic," my mother said. "She'd been warned not to drink while she was pregnant, but she hadn't been able to stop. The doctors told her that if the baby lived, it would be damaged. Fetal alcohol syndrome it's called."

"Did the baby die?" I asked.

"No," my mother told me.

"Did the alcohol hurt it?"

My mother's eyes grew moist and her lower lip trembled.

"Yes," she said softly, "it did. But it could have been much, much worse."

She explained that she and my father had finally convinced Grace to let them call for an ambulance and that she'd stayed behind in the little apartment while my father took Grace to the hospital. Before Grace was carried out of the apartment on the stretcher and loaded into the ambulance, my mother told me, she leaned over Grace and whispered, "You be me." Then she placed her wallet in Grace's hands and kissed her good-bye.

I didn't understand.

"Why did you say, 'You be me'?" I asked. "And why did you give Grace your whole wallet, instead of just giving her some of the money out of it?"

My mother began to cry.

"Do you want me to tell the rest?" my father asked her gently.

But she shook her head, dried her eyes, and continued.

"I wanted a baby more than anything in the world," she told me. "We had tried forever."

"I know," I said. "You've told me a million times how you spent years knitting little booties and sweaters, and then when I finally came, the clothes were all moth-eaten and I couldn't wear them."

My mother got a faraway look in her eyes.

"You were so tiny," she said, "but you had quite a pair of lungs. You could wail all night, and for weeks you did, too. I'd wrap you up tight, and rock you and sing to you until you finally fell asleep. Poor little thing, you had a hard time of it in the beginning."

I had heard all of this before. I knew that I'd come earlier than expected and that I'd been so small and fragile, I looked like a tiny baby bird—all pink and wrinkled. I'd seen pictures of my scrunched-up little self, swaddled in a blanket and cradled in my mother's arms. But I didn't understand why we were going back over all of this now.

"We'd waited so long," my mother continued, "I couldn't believe you were really mine. I couldn't believe I was finally—"

"You haven't finished the story," I interrupted impatiently. "What happened to Grace and the baby? And where was Uncle Mike?"

My mother seemed lost in thought. When she didn't

answer my questions, my father stepped in.

"Your uncle Mike was in jail," he said, "and he still is."

This news came as a shock.

"What did he do?" I asked.

"That's neither here nor there, Bena," he told me. Then he picked up the thread of the story where my mother had left off.

"I rode in the ambulance with Grace," he explained, "and when we got to the hospital, I told them I was the baby's father so that they would let me go in with Grace while she had the baby."

"Did she have a little boy or a little girl?" I asked.

"A sweet little girl," my father said. "No heavier than a sack of flour."

"Willow," my mother said softly. "That's what Grace said she would have called her."

"What do you mean, *would have*?" I said. "I thought you said the baby didn't die."

"She didn't," my mother said. "Though it was touch and go there for a while. Remember, Tom?"

"Of course I remember," he said reaching across me to pat my mother's hand.

"Where is she now?" I asked. "Where is Willow?"

My mother smiled at me, but her eyes were full of

tears again and some of them spilled out and ran down her smooth, wide cheeks.

"She's here, Sugarpea. With us where she belongs."

I felt as if the world had stopped spinning and time was standing still as I struggled to understand what I'd just heard.

"*Me?*" I asked.

My mother nodded.

"You."

"I was there when you came into the world," my father said. "I was the first one to hold you in my arms. But it was your mother who saw you through those first few difficult weeks. She never left your side."

I was confused.

"What happened to the other baby?" I asked my mother. "The one that *you* had?"

"There was no other baby," she said. "People couldn't tell, because of my weight. Everybody knew we'd been trying; they just assumed we'd decided to keep it a secret."

"When we brought you home, they kidded us about how we'd pulled the wool over their eyes." My father laughed.

I was so shocked I could barely breathe. My mother took my hand and squeezed it.

"I wanted a baby more than life itself, Verbie, but I couldn't do it myself. So Grace did it for me. That's why I send her a picture every year. It seems like the least I can do to let her see who you've become."

I could hear my mother's voice, but I wasn't listening to the words anymore. No wonder I'd been feeling so mixed up and mean inside. Mike Colter was bad news, trouble from the get-go, warped, and it was his good-for-nothing blood that was running through my veins. After all these years of thinking I was somebody I wasn't, the real me had finally decided to show up.

CHAPTER THREE

My Annie

Annie was the first person I told. It was the week before Christmas break, a few days before my birthday, and I remember we were standing together out on the playground at school in our winter coats.

"Lots of people are adopted, Verbie," she said. "Are you going to try to meet your real parents? I'd be dying to know what they were like if I were you."

"They're not my real parents, and I don't ever want to meet them," I said angrily.

"You don't have to take my head off," said Annie defensively. "I was just asking."

"Why would I want to meet them? Grace practically pickled me before I was born. And Mike Colter is in jail—*for killing someone.*"

My father hadn't wanted to tell me what Mike Colter had done to get himself put in jail, but I had insisted I had a right to know everything after having been kept in the dark for so long. Finally he gave in and told me that there'd been some sort of a fight, and that Mike had pushed a man so hard it broke his neck.

"I know what you're doing, Verbie. You're telling me all this stuff now to make me feel guilty about not coming to your birthday party this year," Annie said.

"No I'm not," I told her. "I'm scared, Annie. Scared I'm going to end up being like Mike Colter."

It was starting to snow. Annie patted her pockets, looking for her mittens. When she didn't find them, she began blowing on her fingers to warm them up.

"That's just crazy talk," she said. "We both know you wouldn't hurt a fly, Verbie."

"I'm not the same person I used to be."

"You look the same," she said.

She didn't understand. Nobody understood. My parents said that the reason they hadn't told me the truth was because they didn't want me to worry, but I'd been worrying all year that there was something wrong with me. And now I knew what it was.

The bell rang and Annie and I started walking back toward the school building. Lacy snowflakes, like little white doilies, caught in Annie's dark hair and eyelashes.

"Listen," she said to me, "I'm sorry about your party,

Verbie, really I am, but Heather invited me to go ski-
ing with her family at Holiday Mountain for the whole
week. I have to go—I already bought ski pants and
everything."

Heather Merwin was a stuck-up girl Annie had
never shown any interest in before.

"It's okay," I told her, even though it wasn't.

Best friends were supposed to be there on your
birthday, and they were supposed to know when you
needed them to give you a hug and tell you that everything was going to be all right. I'd thought that Annie
Bingham and I would be best friends forever, but for
the first time I found myself wondering if maybe that
wasn't true.

Annie and I had met on the morning of our first
day in kindergarten, and by the time we went home
that afternoon, we were friends. We did everything
together—rode our bikes, went ice-skating, baked a
million chocolate chip cookies, and had sleepovers
almost every weekend at each other's houses. One of
our favorite activities was collecting things—pinecones,
pretty rocks, bottle caps, it didn't matter. We'd come
back to my room with our pockets stuffed full, sit on
the floor, and spread our treasures out in front of us.

Then we'd choose a winner and two runners-up, like in a beauty pageant. Being best friends with Annie was like breathing; it was part of who I was.

In the beginning of fifth grade, when some of the girls in our class started coming to school wearing makeup and shoes with chunky heels, Annie and I made fun of them for trying to act older than they were. While we swung on the rings or jumped rope at recess, those girls would cluster in tight knots out on the playground whispering and giggling whenever a boy walked by. I remember telling Annie: "If I ever start acting like that, please shoot me." And she laughed and said, "Don't worry, I will."

Then one day Annie bought some lip gloss. "It's just clear, Verbie," she said when she showed it to me, "Like Chapstick only shinier. It's no big deal."

But the lip gloss was only the beginning. Pretty soon, Annie didn't want to have sleepovers anymore. She said that kind of thing was "babyish." Not long after that, she started hanging around with Heather.

My mother always made a big fuss over my birthday, but that day after my conversation with Annie on the playground, I came home from school and told my mother to cancel my birthday party. She tried to talk me out of it; she'd been planning the party for weeks. She was going to make a red velvet cake from scratch and decorate the house with streamers and balloons. She'd already bought candy for the goodie bags and prizes for the party games my friends and I would play.

"A party might be just the thing to lift your spirits," she said.

"I'll run away if you make me do it," I screamed at her. "I'll run away and you'll never see me again!" Then I threw myself down on the couch and cried.

My mother came and sat beside me.

"I'm so sorry you're hurting," she said, stroking my hair softly with her fingers. "If I could take your pain away and put it on myself, you know I would."

That night after I went to bed, my mother called all the people I'd sent invitations to and told them that I'd come down with a bug and didn't feel up to celebrating.

I spent the day of my birthday upstairs lying on my bed staring at the ceiling. There was a pile of presents waiting for me downstairs but I didn't feel like opening them. What I wanted couldn't possibly be inside any of those boxes. Even though I told her not to, my mother made my favorite dinner, steak and french fries, but I didn't touch a bite. After the dinner dishes were cleared, she brought out the red velvet cake she'd made, with eleven white candles in a circle on the top and a twelfth in the middle "to grow on."

"Make a wish, birthday girl," she said as she set the cake down in front of me.

I closed my eyes and took a deep breath. And that was the first time I wished to be somebody other than who I was—somebody other than Verbena Ellen Colter.

CHAPTER FOUR

Lilac Time

I struggled through the rest of the school year, keeping to myself and fighting a secret battle against the rotten forces I knew were at work inside me. I'd already lost Annie. After the Christmas ski trip, she and Heather had become even closer. By Easter the two of them were as intertwined as the milky stems of the dandelions Annie and I had spent hours together weaving into chains. The cherry on top of my fifth-grade year was seeing Chris Cartwright holding hands with Annie out in the parking lot right before the graduation ceremony. My parents and I had just gotten out of the car when my mother gasped and pointed.

"Is that *your* Annie with the Cartwright boy?" she whispered.

But it wasn't my Annie. Not anymore.

* * *

For some mysterious reason that spring the lilac bush in our front yard bloomed late. After the graduation ceremony, as my parents and I climbed out of the car, the air was heavy with the sweet scent of lilac, and the full branches arched out of the bush like rockets shooting off purple sprays of fireworks. My mother held the camera in her hand, the black plastic strap tight around her wrist.

"What do you say we take the photo in front of the lilacs this year, Verbie? We might as well take advantage of this late bloom. It may never happen again."

It had always been a tradition in my family for me to pose for a photograph on the first and last day of every school year. My mother, an avid scrapbooker, pasted the photos into a big book with a cover decorated to look like a blackboard, the words *School Daze* written on it in chalk. Apparently she'd also been sending copies of the photos to Grace Kincaid, and although she'd never received a reply, the cards hadn't been returned either.

"I don't want to have my picture taken," I grumbled.

I had read up on fetal alcohol syndrome and knew now that in addition to my small size and learning difficulties, the damage Grace Kincaid's drinking had caused included my bad eyesight and the unusual smoothness of the space between my upper lip and my nose. I felt hideous.

"Come here, Sugarpea," my mother called to me as she rummaged in her purse in search of a comb. "We need to tidy you up a bit first."

"I just told you, I don't want you to take my picture," I said. "And I don't want you to call me Sugarpea anymore either. It's *babyish*."

All I wanted was to get inside and take my shoes off. There were two painful blisters the size of dimes on the backs of my heels—the price I was paying for having ignored my mother's suggestion to try on my black shoes the day before to make sure they still fit.

"Just give it a quick once-over," my mother said, holding the comb out to me.

"*No picture*," I told her, pushing my glasses up with a bent knuckle and then pulling them partway back down my nose again.

My mother looked at my feet and frowned.

"Are those shoes pinching?" she asked.

I hadn't told her the shoes were too small.

"There's nothing wrong with my shoes," I said, gritting my teeth so hard my jaw hurt. I didn't want to lose my temper. Ever since I'd found out the truth about who I really was, I'd been trying to control the angry feelings I had inside, trying to keep the rotten part of me from taking over.

"These pictures are a tradition in our family, Sugarpea," my mother said.

"Not anymore," I told her, still gritting my teeth. "And how many times do I have to tell you—*stop calling me Sugarpea.*"

Exasperated, my mother turned to my father.

"Can you please talk to her, Tom?"

"I'll do my best," he told her.

My father came over and put his arm around me.

"Bena," he said, giving my shoulder a little squeeze.

I sighed and pushed his arm away. I knew what he was going to say. He always took her side.

"You know how your mother feels about those scrapbooks of hers. Why all this fuss over one little picture?"

"She's the one who's making the fuss," I said.

"Someday you'll be glad to have a picture to help you to remember this time in your life," my mother called from across the yard.

Red-hot anger rose inside me like lava in a volcano. Didn't she know this had been the worst year of my life?

Not only had I lost my best friend, I had lost myself as well.

"One little picture, Bena, that's all she's asking," my father said.

It took everything I had, but in the end I managed to push my anger back down inside long enough to let my mother take my picture in front of the lilac bush. But I can't look at it now without feeling a pang. I remember what I was thinking about as the shutter clicked.

My mother volunteered at the Sullivan County Humane Society. The vet at the shelter was a man named Dr. Finn, and he knew my mother had a soft spot for stray animals, particularly the ones with the saddest stories. He'd call her up to ask if she could come take a look at some poor unfortunate creature someone had brought into the clinic or left in a cardboard box on his doorstep in the middle of the night. Once she was there, he would ask her if she'd be willing to foster the animal "just for a little while," until it either died or recovered enough to be put up for adoption. He knew perfectly well that any animal my mother agreed to take home was going to end up living out whatever was left of its life in her care. Teddy was the one exception.

He was a big dog—a boxer-shepherd mix—brown and sleek and strong. He had seemed friendly at first, wagging his tail and licking everybody's face. But deep down inside, it turned out Teddy was mean. He got into fights with the other animals in the house, and if you came anywhere near him when he was eating, he'd not only growl at you, he'd snap. I was just a toddler when Teddy came to live with us, a little girl who didn't know better than to try to hug a dog while it was eating its dinner. So he bit me. I still have a crescent-shaped scar on my wrist to prove it. First thing the next morning, my mother put Teddy in the car and drove him back to the shelter. We never talked about what happened to him after that.

It was Teddy I was thinking about that day as I posed for my mother in front of the lilacs. I was wondering if his meanness had showed from the outside, or if, like mine, it was hidden in his blood like poison. My memory of Teddy was foggy—I was only three years old when he bit me—but my mother kept a scrapbook of pictures of all the animals we'd taken in, and it occurred to me that maybe there would be a picture of Teddy in there.

Later that same afternoon when my mother left the house to go into town on an errand, I went into the den to find that scrapbook. *Friends "Fur"-Ever* it said on the cover, which was decorated with little paw prints. I searched every page for a picture of Teddy, and when I didn't find one, I began to go through the loose photographs my mother kept in shoe boxes on the tall shelves that lined the walls of the room.

Scrapbooking had overtaken the den. Everywhere you looked there was an explosion of colored ribbons, or shiny strips of border papers decorated with stickers. There were plastic bins bursting with decals and rubber stamps, and on a folding card table sat a giant paper cutter surrounded by coffee cans jammed full of scissors and markers. The scrapbooks themselves, bound in blue leather, occupied two whole sets of shelves in the room, and the floor was so littered with confetti—tiny cutout shapes of bears, kittens, and hearts from the paper punches she used—it looked like a circus parade had passed through.

I didn't find any pictures of Teddy in the shoe boxes. I wasn't sure if that was because he'd been with us for such a short time that no photographs were ever taken, or if my mother had decided not to keep any pictures of Teddy because she felt bad about what had happened to him. As I was leaving the room, I glanced up and something caught my eye. On top of one of the sets of shelves lay a flat white box tied with a red string. I'd never noticed it before, and curious to see what was inside, I ran and got the stepstool from the kitchen.

The box wasn't very heavy, and once I got it down I was surprised to find my name written across the top in my mother's careful handwriting. When I untied the string and opened the box, I discovered it was full of little pieces of me I was not even aware that my mother had been saving. There was a lock of my hair, a plastic box containing several baby teeth I'd left under my pillow for the tooth fairy, a note to Santa painstakingly printed in block letters with red crayon, and in the very bottom of the box, carefully wrapped in white tissue paper, the little peapod dress. My mother had fished it out of the throwaway pile, unable to bear the thought of some other little girl wearing it.

I had just lifted the dress from the box when I heard my mother's car coming up the driveway. Quickly I put everything back where I had found it and managed to be standing out in the kitchen drinking a glass of milk by the time my mother walked in the door carrying a bag of groceries in her arms.

"I've got your favorite. Orange Popsicles," she said as she set the bag down on the counter. She had not changed out of the peapod dress she'd worn to the graduation ceremony that morning, and as I looked at her standing there smiling at me, I was so sad for both of us I wanted to cry.

"You're having a hard day, aren't you?" she said. "Would a Popsicle help?"

I wanted to run to her and bury my face in her warm neck. I wanted to tell her how sorry I was that I was ugly and small and mean. How sorry I was that instead of the perfect little girl she'd always dreamed of having, she'd ended up with me. Instead I asked her a question.

"Why did you send Teddy away?"

She seemed surprised.

"Teddy?"

"Why didn't you give him a second chance after he bit me?" I asked.

She stood still and thought about it for a moment.

"Teddy couldn't help being the way he was," she said, "but mean is mean, and no amount of nice can fix it."

Mean is mean. The words echoed in my head. Didn't my mother realize when she said that no amount of nice could fix what was wrong with Teddy, she might as well have been talking about me?

CHAPTER FIVE

Doghouse

My summers had always revolved around spending time with Annie. As soon as school let out, we would put our heads together and come up with a project. One summer we made a fort, complete with curtains and real shingles on the roof. Another time we set up a little flower stand on the sidewalk in front of the post office and sold bouquets of Queen Anne's lace and black-eyed Susans that we'd gathered in the big meadow behind Annie's house.

That summer between fifth and sixth grade, Annie and her new best friend, Heather, had decided to be junior counselors at a Y camp in the Poconos. Although I was relieved that I would be spared the sight of them whispering and giggling together for two whole months, I wasn't sure what I was going to do with myself without Annie to keep me company.

For the first few days of vacation I hung around at home reading and watching TV and not even bothering to get dressed. Sometimes, when I started feeling stir-crazy, I'd go out in the backyard and throw a ball for Jack.

Like all the dogs we ever had, Jack came to us from the shelter. Somebody had found him lying in the road. He was in terrible shape, his back left leg so badly broken Dr. Finn had to operate and take it off. When nobody showed up to claim him, my mother agreed to foster him at home, and he'd been ours ever since. He was a great dog, bighearted and friendly. His only shortcoming was a passion for chasing skunks, which meant there was a permanent stink to him that no amount of tomato juice or peppermint soap could get out. My father built him a doghouse out in the yard so he wouldn't smell up the house, but my mother always took pity on him and let Jack come inside anyway.

Ever since school had let out, my mother had been driving me crazy trying to come up with "fun" things we could do together—planting a rock garden, making strawberry jam—but I didn't feel like doing anything, especially not with her. Everything she did and said rubbed me the wrong way, and when she didn't let up, I would lose my temper.

Sometimes I said hurtful things, sometimes I just yelled. I always felt bad afterward, but what did she expect? She'd said it herself: Mean is mean, and no amount of nice can fix it.

"Fourth of July's coming up, Verbie. Why don't we drive over to Pennsylvania and get some sparklers? We could pick up a couple of sandwiches at that wonderful little deli in Riley and eat lunch down by the river," she suggested one day while she was unloading the dishwasher.

"I'm too old for sparklers," I told her, biting at a hangnail on my thumb.

"Are you too old for ham and cheese too?" she teased.

"No, but what's the point of driving all the way to Pennsylvania to get a sandwich you could make for yourself in two minutes at home?"

"What about trying to line up some babysitting work?" she said. "Summer people are always looking for sitters, and I hear they pay very well."

"I don't like babies," I told her, "or flatlanders."

"*Verbena,*" my mother scolded, "you know how I feel about that word."

Flatlander was an unflattering term the locals used

to describe the summer people who came up to the Catskill Mountains from New York City to vacation. Flatlanders drove expensive cars, threw cash around like Monopoly money, and turned their noses up at the cheese selection in the deli case at Peck's. Nobody liked them, but everybody pretended to. My father said that was because people in Clydesdale knew which side their bread was buttered on.

"Everybody else calls them flatlanders," I said. "Why shouldn't I?"

My mother pulled a fistful of clean silverware out of the dishwasher and carried it like a bouquet over to the drawer.

"Maybe Dr. Finn could find you something to do at the shelter," she said, returning to the subject of my nonexistent summer plans. "I'm going over there tomorrow afternoon to see about a nest of bunnies somebody turned over with a mower. Poor little things got their ears—"

"Stop!" I cried, putting my hand up. "I don't want to hear about the bunnies."

"There were five to begin with," my mother said, closing the silverware drawer with her hip, "but only two are left."

She reached into a box of cheese crackers that was

sitting open on the counter and popped a few into her mouth.

"I told you I didn't want to hear about the bunnies, Mom."

I was sitting on the couch in the family room, off the kitchen, still in my nightgown. There were Sunday morning cartoons flickering on the television with the sound turned off. My mother came over and stood behind me, resting her hands on my shoulders. There was orange cheese-cracker dust on her fingers.

"How about some pancakes—would that cheer you up?" she asked.

"I'm not hungry!" I shouted, shrugging out from under her touch. "And I'm not going to be hungry ten minutes from now when you ask me again, either."

"You might feel better if you got some fresh air. Moping around in your pj's all day isn't going to help anything, Sugarpea."

"I don't want to get some fresh air. I want to be left alone," I said. "And how many more times do I have to tell you—*don't call me Sugarpea.*"

"I've called you that name since you were a baby, Verbena," my mother said.

"Well in case you haven't noticed, I'm not a baby anymore."

I was so mad I couldn't even look at her. Everything about my mother annoyed me, including her weight, which had ballooned to an all-time high. I knew it was mean, but the fact of the matter was I was embarrassed to even be seen with her. If only she would leave me alone. But no matter where I went, she always seemed to be hovering nearby asking me questions or trying to get me to eat something.

My father must have heard us arguing, because he appeared in the doorway, holding a wooden bird feeder in his hand.

"Everything all right in here, ladies?" he asked.

Sunday was his only day off, so he'd been out in his workshop happily hammering away all morning. He had a quiet way of tracking the storms between my mother and me without ever quite being drawn into them.

"Everything's fine," my mother said. "We've just been talking about what Verbie might like to do with her free time this summer."

"I could use a hand out in the shop. This feeder is about ready for a coat of paint, and there's a brush out there with a certain little girl's name on it."

My mother wasn't the only one who could set me off.

"Little girl?" I said. *"Little girl?"*

My father looked to my mother, who turned her hands palms up.

I felt like the monkey in a game of monkey in the middle.

"I'm going up to my room to read," I said, getting off the couch.

"Do you have a good book?" my mother asked, springing into full-blown fuss mode. "'Cause if you need one, we can go into town and swing by the library—no wait, it's not open today. We'll see if they have anything at Peck's instead—a paperback, or maybe you'd like a magazine. Afterward we can stop and get manicures. I'll give Trudy a call and see if she can fit us in."

She reached for the phone, and before I could stop it, the lava overflowed inside me and I was yelling again.

"What's the matter with you? Are you crazy? I didn't say I wanted to go to town with you. Why would I want to go anywhere with you? Look at what you've got on. You look like you're wearing a tent. I guess that's what happens when you sit around all day eating cheese crackers."

"That's no way to speak to your mother, young

lady," my father said sternly. "You go up to your room this instant."

"That's what I was trying to do in the first place, *remember*?" I said. Then I stormed upstairs to my room in a huff, slamming the door behind me so hard it made the walls shake.

My father was smart enough to retreat to his workshop out of the line of fire for the rest of that morning, but my mother couldn't help herself. Five minutes after I'd been sent to my room, she was upstairs telling me to come back down. I apologized to her for what I'd said. I was truly sorry. Not only for hurting her but for judging her as well. I knew better, but hard as I tried, I just couldn't seem to control my temper. My mother accepted my apology, but as soon as I got downstairs and settled in front of the television again, she started buzzing around me like a gnat.

"Can I get you anything? A glass of juice? Pancakes?"

"For the millionth time, Mom," I told her, *"I'm not hungry."*

My mother frowned and put the back of her hand to my forehead.

"You feel a little warm," she said. "I'll make you some Jell-O."

I couldn't stand it any longer, so I turned off the television and went outside.

Jack was in his favorite spot, cooling his belly in the dirt under the clothesline. Crooking my pinkie, I slipped it between my lips and whistled. Jack lifted his head, wagged his tail, and struggled awkwardly to his feet. He could walk and run as well as any other dog, but with only three legs, getting up was kind of hard for him.

I whistled again and Jack came over, dipping his head and bumping my hand with his nose to try to get me to pet him.

"P.U.," I said, waving my hand in front of my face. "No pats for you, Stinkerbell."

A mourning dove flew by, landing with a clatter on a feeder hanging from the limb of a crabapple tree. There wasn't a tree in our yard that didn't have at least one of my father's bird feeders dangling from its branches. He always kept them filled—black oilers for the chickadees, doves, and nuthatches, thistle seed for the finches, and greasy blocks of glistening white suet for the jays and woodpeckers. He'd even made a squirrel feeder, with an ear of corn stuck on a post and a glass jar full of peanuts.

The garage door was open. Looking in at my bike,

I thought about taking a ride, but where would I go? Annie and I would sometimes ride down the hill into town to watch the volunteer firemen play softball behind the firehouse, but I didn't feel like doing that by myself.

I heard a car coming up the road. Dietz Road is a dead-end street, and since ours was the only house on it (except for the Allen house, which hadn't been occupied in years), I figured it was either one of my mother's nutty scrapbooking friends coming to swap stickers and rubber stamps or a customer wanting to talk to my dad about a job. I was surprised when, instead of turning into our driveway, the unfamiliar blue station wagon drove right past, kicking up dust and gravel behind it. A woman in dark sunglasses and a floppy hat with a wide brim gripped the wheel, staring straight ahead, and I caught a glimpse of a face pressed up against the glass in the backseat. For a split second I thought it was a dog, but then I realized it was a boy with reddish hair, the exact same color as Jack's fur.

When the car reached the end of the road, those people, whoever they were, would realize their mistake and have no choice but to turn around and come back down, I thought. But fifteen minutes later when the blue station wagon still hadn't returned, I began to wonder if something had happened.

I hadn't bothered to get dressed yet that day, but I didn't feel like taking the time to go inside and change. Besides, I didn't want to risk another argument with my mother. I looked down at my nightgown, which was sleeveless and white, and decided that if you didn't know any better, you might mistake it for a sundress.

"Come on, Jackie boy," I said, "Let's go." Then I wheeled my bike out of the garage and, with Jack trotting along beside me, pedaled off up the road.

CHAPTER SIX

Hide and Seek

It didn't take long to find the blue station wagon. It was parked in the driveway of the Allen house. To my surprise the woman in the big hat was unloading suitcases and boxes from the back. Curious, I got off my bike, stashed it in the weeds, and quietly crept closer to get a better look at her. *Flatlander,* I said to myself as soon as I saw her tight black clothes and the shiny gold bracelets decorating her arms halfway up to her elbows. Her hair was blond, a brassy shade of yellow I was sure had come from a bottle, and she was thin as a pencil. She wore very high heels with leather straps that criss-crossed around her ankles like ribbons on a Christmas package. I would have been willing to bet there wasn't a person in all of Sullivan County who owned a pair of shoes like that.

As the woman pulled the last of the suitcases out of

the car, she must have tugged too hard on the handle, because it broke off, sending the heavy bag crashing down onto the toe of one of her fancy shoes. She grabbed her foot and started hopping up and down, cursing a blue streak. When the worst of the pain had passed, she stopped hopping, lifted her head, and yelled at the top of her lungs.

"*Pooch!*"

One of the second-floor windows of the Allen house flew open and a boy stuck his head out. I recognized the face as the one I'd seen earlier, pressed up against the car window.

"Coming!" he called down, then ducked his head back inside and disappeared.

A faded FOR RENT sign was nailed to a large tree in the yard, but nobody had lived in the Allen house for years. The real estate office that handled it hired my father's company to keep the lawn mowed, but other than that, the house was in poor condition. It was badly in need of a fresh coat of paint, and I noticed that several of the shutters had fallen off.

"Mountain retreat, my butt," the woman grumbled as she pushed the suitcase with the broken handle over to the edge of the lawn and left it there along with the rest of the stuff she'd already unloaded. When she closed the rear hatch of the car, she slammed it so hard that Jack, who was standing near the bottom of the driveway, barked.

"What the—"

Startled, the woman turned and seemed to look right at me, but I must have been well hidden by the weeds, because slowly she shifted her gaze to the left until she spotted Jack. Without taking her eyes off him, she yelled again.

"*Pooch!*"

"I'm right here, Mom."

The redheaded boy had come out onto the porch and was standing on the top step with his hands on his hips. Despite the summer heat he was wearing long pants—the baggy kind with lots of pockets—and a long-sleeved shirt.

"Where's Dixie?" the woman asked anxiously.

"Upstairs," answered the boy.

She turned and looked at him with narrowed eyes.

"Are you sure?"

He nodded, and the woman went back to staring down the driveway at Jack.

"Bring me a stick," she called over her shoulder.

The boy obeyed, running down the steps and quickly picking up a couple of small twigs, which he brought to her.

"What am I supposed to do with these?" she asked, dropping the twigs on the ground, "Bring me something bigger."

"What's it for?" he asked.

She pointed down the driveway at Jack.

"I don't like the looks of that dog," she said.

The boy put his hand over his eyes to shield them from the sun. "He looks friendly to me. He's wagging his tail, see?"

Jack started up the driveway dipping his head, coming to say hello, but as soon as he got within full view, the woman gasped.

"I told you there was something wrong with that dog," she said. "Look at him—he's missing a leg. Some wild animal probably chewed it off. What if he's got rabies?"

The boy shook his head.

"If he had rabies, he'd be foaming at the mouth, Mom. Besides he's wearing a collar. He must belong to somebody around here."

"Who in their right mind would want a dog like that for a pet? He ought to be put to sleep. Git!" the woman yelled at Jack.

Jack stopped in his tracks and tilted his head, confused by her unfriendly tone.

"I said *git*," she shouted again.

When Jack still didn't move, she picked up a stone and threw it at him, clipping him in the side. He yelped and jumped back. When she bent down to pick up another stone, Jack finally got the message, tucked tail, and slunk back down the driveway.

"The last thing I need is to get bitten by some rabid hillbilly dog," the woman grumbled, dropping the stone.

"I told you, Mom. Rabies makes you foam at the mouth," the boy said. "And then you go crazy and die."

"Thank you, Doctor Doom," his mother said. She touched her cheek with her fingertips and grimaced. "I need a pain pill and an icepack. Help me get this stuff inside. I think I'm starting to swell again."

When the boy didn't move, his mother got annoyed.

"What's the holdup, Pooch?"

"I was just wondering," he said. "Do you think it's true, what that lady at the post office said about the house?"

The woman waved his question away like she was shooing a fly.

"Of course not. She was just trying to get a rise out of you, Pooch. Fun is hard to come by in a podunk town like this. Can you imagine having to live here year-round? I'd rather die. They don't even have high-speed internet up here—they use dial-up. *Dial-up.* Now come on, help me get this stuff inside before I puff up."

I'd never heard the word *podunk* before, but it didn't take a genius to know that it was an insult. Typical. Flatlanders always thought they were better than everybody else.

I stayed hidden in the weeds watching until the boy and his mother had lugged the last of their stuff up the stairs and into the house. When they were finished, the boy came back out and sat on the porch by himself for a while. *Pooch.* Could that really be his name, I wondered? And why had they come to Clydesdale if they thought it was such an awful place? One thing I didn't have to wonder about, though, was what it was they'd heard down at the post office. Francine, the postmistress, loved to gossip. When she learned where the newcomers were staying, she would have been eager to pass along what everyone in town had been saying for years . . . *the Allen house was haunted.*

CHAPTER SEVEN

Muziky-Muziky

Tracy Allen was the youngest of the three Allen girls. The summer she turned nine, she and her family went on a picnic down at Bonners Lake. Tracy was a good swimmer—she'd earned her deep-water badge at the community pool in Washerville just like her sisters—but that day down at Bonners Lake, she drowned.

Nobody knows exactly what happened. Maybe she got a cramp, or maybe she dove too deep and hit her head on rock. All anybody could say for sure was that one minute she was there, and the next minute she was gone forever. I was only a baby when Tracy Allen died, so I never knew her, but I'd heard the story a million times. When something tragic like that happens in a small town, it never quite goes away.

The Allens moved away soon after the accident, and it wasn't long before the rumors started up about the house being haunted. People claimed to have seen Tracy's ghost sitting in the window, and some even said they'd heard her crying and calling out for help in the middle of the night.

It was because of Tracy Allen that I refused to take swimming lessons when I was little.

"Swimming is fun, Verbie," my mother told me, "and besides, it's not safe for a person not to know how to swim. You're six years old now. Plenty old enough to learn how to swim."

But Tracy Allen had learned how to swim, and look what had happened to her.

In spite of my protests, my mother insisted that I take lessons at the community pool. I spent the first three classes clinging to her legs sobbing. Eventually, after much coaxing by both the swim instructor and my mother, I was persuaded to get into the shallow end of the pool, where after a good deal more coaxing I finally managed to master the dog paddle well enough to take me, kicking and spluttering, from one side of the pool to the other. By that time the other kids in the class, Annie among them, had moved into the deep end to learn how to tread water in preparation for the deep-water test, but I dug in my heels. Although I was no longer afraid of getting into the pool, and could not only dog paddle but also float on my back, the thought of being in water over my head threw me into such a panic that I think everyone just decided to be satisfied with what I had already achieved and leave it at that.

As I pedaled home in my nightgown that summer afternoon after spying on the new neighbors moving into the Allen house, I wondered what kind of people threw stones at innocent dogs who were only trying to be friendly. Flatlanders, that's who. If they hated Clydesdale so much, why didn't they turn around and go back where they'd come from?

Jack beat me home and was back in his favorite spot under the clothesline when I arrived. Inside, my dad was napping on the couch, with the newspaper over his face. There was a peanut butter and grape jelly sandwich waiting for me on the counter, and next to it a note from my mother saying that she'd gone into town for an emergency band practice.

My mother played in the Clydesdale Band. It wasn't much of a claim to fame, since anybody who knew how to play an instrument even halfway decently was allowed to be in the band. She sat in the middle, in between the clarinets and the flutes and right behind the trombones.

It was easy to spot her, not only because of her size but also because she was the only one in the band who played the spoons. When she played at home she used our regular everyday silverware, but on concert nights she always used a pair of silver soup spoons, holding them together back to back, making them click in time to the music by tapping them against a little padded block of wood that my father had wired onto an old snare drum stand.

Clydesdale was very proud of its band, but nobody had much time to practice, so the music always sounded a little rough around the edges. That didn't stop people from coming to the concerts, though. Not just summer people either—town people came too. Everybody brought blankets or lawn chairs to sit on and cans of *Off!* to keep the mosquitoes and no-see-ums from biting. If it was raining, people would park in front of the post office and along both sides of the road. Then they'd sit in their cars with the windows cracked open, honking at the end of each number instead of applauding.

The summer concerts were on Wednesday nights, and sometimes the band would get together earlier in the day to run the numbers a couple of times, but this was a Sunday, so I had a feeling the reason my mother had called it an *emergency* practice was because the band was scrambling to get ready for the Fourth of July.

The Clydesdale Band always played at the Fourth of July celebration. There would be barbecued chicken, a strawberry shortcake raffle with proceeds going to the ladies' auxiliary, and after the concert a small fireworks display. Annie and I had always watched the fireworks together, lying on our backs on an old blue bedspread. We would each hold our breath in anticipation as the rockets shot up, then whoop and shriek as they exploded into patterns we gave names to, like waterfall, curly fry, and dandelion puff. I had never missed a Fourth of July celebration in my life, but I'd already made up my mind that I wasn't going that year. I knew the old blue bedspread would feel as big as the ocean without Annie lying beside me.

I poured myself a glass of cold milk and ate my sandwich standing up at the counter. Nearby, two spoons lay near a jar of silver polish and the rag my mother had used to shine them that morning in preparation for the upcoming concert. I picked up one of the shiny spoons and was making a face at my upside-down reflection when Honey came over and began rubbing against my legs, meowing. I reached down and scratched her between the ears, but we both knew it wasn't me she'd come looking for.

Most of the animals my mother brought home from the shelter were too sick or too old or too sad to get better. She cared for them anyway, and gave them names, and did her best to make them comfortable until their time was up. Over the years a parade of abandoned pets had come through our house, but from a very early age I got good at being able to tell which ones it wasn't safe to love. I thought Honey was one of those, but she ended up surprising me.

I was four years old when my mother brought her home. One of the grocery clerks at Peck's had discovered the tiny kitten curled up behind the soda can machine in the recycling shed.

"Where is the mama cat?" I asked.

"Nobody knows," my mother told me.

"What if she comes back looking for her baby?"

"I don't think that's going to happen, Sugarpea."

"Why not?"

"Sometimes the mama rejects a baby if it isn't perfect."

"What's not perfect?" I asked, peering at the little ball of golden fluff in my mother's hands.

She gently pulled up one of the kitten's eyelids, revealing a milky white eye. "She's blind," she told me. "See?"

I shuddered and hid my face in my hands.

Dr. Finn explained to my mother that because the kitten was so young—in addition to being blind— the chances of her surviving without her mother were slim to none.

"The most humane thing would probably be to put her down, Ellen," he said. But he knew my mother wouldn't let him do that.

Instead she brought the kitten home and made a little bed for her with a heating pad in it, and she got up every two hours all night long for weeks to feed her warm milk with an eyedropper.

"I'll be your mama now," I remember hearing my mother croon to the tiny kitten once as she held her up against her cheek.

After a while Honey, which is what my mother decided to call her because of her color and her sweet temperament, was strong enough to stand up and lap milk from a saucer if we put it down right in front of her and dipped a finger in to help lead her mouth to it. She would never be able to hunt mice or chase yarn balls the way other cats could, but no matter where my mother went in the house, somehow Honey could always manage to find her.

I poured what was left of my glass of milk into Honey's dish and set it down in the corner.

"Here you go, kittycat," I said.

I watched Honey make her way across the room. Stepping carefully, her eyelids closed tight, she looked as if she were sleepwalking. I pushed my glasses up with a knuckle and pulled them partway back down.

My father was still asleep on the couch, snoring loudly. I looked up at the clock, which was shaped like a teapot and hung on a nail above the stove. It was only twelve thirty. How was I going to fill the long afternoon ahead? I found myself thinking about that boy, Pooch. If only someone else had moved into the Allen house instead—a nice girl my age, for instance.

I got an apple out of the fridge and went back outside. Band practice never lasted very long. My mother would be home soon. If I didn't want to risk another exhibition of my true nature, I was going to have to find something to do other than hang around the house all afternoon. I had left my bike out in the driveway, so I wheeled it back into the garage. That's when I noticed the fishing poles leaning up against the wall in a corner. And suddenly I knew exactly how I was going to spend the rest of my afternoon.

CHAPTER EIGHT

My Treasure

It was my father who taught me how to fish. By the time I was four, I knew how to thread a night crawler onto a hook to get the most mileage out of it and how to catch a catfish by tying lead sinkers to the line so the bait would dangle down near the bottom. Bonners Lake was about a quarter of a mile away from our house, and sometimes when I was younger, my father would wake me up early in the morning before he left for work and we'd go fishing there together.

My mother didn't like our little fishing trips. Even though it was one of the only things my father and I ever did alone together, she felt jealous and left out. If she could possibly have come with us, she would have, but she had bad knees, and the only way to get down to the lake was on foot, down a steep path that wound through the woods. She would try to stall our departure as long as possible by insisting on coating every inch of me with sunscreen and bug spray, and tucking and retucking my pant legs into my socks to protect me from tick bites. She would tell us to watch out for poison ivy and water snakes and whatever else she could think of, but the final warning was always the same—"Don't take your eyes off her, Tom. Not even for a second. You remember what happened to that little Allen girl."

My mother was afraid that I might drown in the lake the way Tracy Allen had, but I wasn't worried about that at all. A person can't drown if they don't go in the water. In the pool in Washerville, there was a nylon rope with blue plastic floats tied to it separating the shallow end from the deep end. It was easy to tell where the water would be over my head. But Bonners Lake was dark and murky and you couldn't see the bottom at all. There was no way of telling how deep it was, or where it might drop off, which is why I had never gone swimming there. And I never planned to either.

Bluegill and perch would practically jump onto our hooks the minute my father and I put them in the water, and if we were willing to put up with the inconvenience of tangled lines and lost lures, sometimes there were pike and bass lurking in the weedy spots. I enjoyed those fishing trips with my dad, but as his business took off, he had less and less free time, and pretty soon the poles began to gather dust out in the garage. A couple of years back Annie and I had come across them one day when we were bored and looking for something to do. We'd asked my mother if it was okay for us to go fishing together.

"Absolutely not," she'd said. "I don't want you girls anywhere near that lake by yourselves."

But I was older now, almost twelve. Old enough to go fishing by myself, whether my mother thought so or not. And best of all, I knew that she couldn't follow me there, so at least for the afternoon I could let down my guard and not have to worry about losing my temper.

I'd hiked up my nightgown, and was down on my hands and knees in the flower bed digging for worms to use for bait, when I heard the sound of a car approaching. Hopping up onto the speckled rock, I looked down the hill and recognized my mother's car, raising a plume of gray dust behind it. Band practice was over. I had planned to change out of my nightgown into a pair of shorts and a T-shirt before heading out, but there wouldn't be time now. My mother would be home any minute. I ran inside, tiptoed past my sleeping father, and scribbled a note saying that I'd gone for a walk—which was the truth, just not the whole truth. I noticed there was a little breeze coming through the open window, so I anchored the note to the counter with one of the silver spoons. By the time my mother's car started up the driveway, I was already in the woods following the path down to Bonners Lake.

Jack decided to tag along, but after a while he picked up the scent of something I sincerely hoped wouldn't turn out to have a white stripe running down its back, and took off. Even on only three legs he was fast, quickly disappearing into the bushes. I was barefoot and my progress was hampered by the nightgown, which billowed out around my ankles as I moved, snagging on the prickers and blackberry brambles that grew along the edges of the path. Eventually I got tired of having to stop and work the tiny thorns out of the fabric and took to yanking myself free, which quickly reduced the hem to tatters. I wasn't worried, though—it was an old nightgown, and I had plenty of others at home.

Near the end of the path, the trees began to thin and the undergrowth changed from brown to green. As I stepped out of the cool woods into the heat and light of the day, the air was completely still. Without even a wisp of breeze to ripple it, Bonners Lake stretched out before me like a giant sheet of green glass. Jack barked in the distance. I saw what looked like a promising skipper, bent down, and picked it up. Wrapping my finger around the curve of the flat stone, I cocked my arm back and skimmed it out across the smooth surface of the water—one, two, three long skips, and then a bunch of smaller ones, too close together to count. When I bent down to pick up another stone, something glistened in the sun near the edge of the lake and caught my eye. At first I thought it was a shiny black rock, until I realized it was actually a turtle sunning itself on a log, and curious to see what kind it was, I crept slowly toward it. As soon as my shadow fell across the water, the turtle slid quickly off the log, disappearing with a soft *plop.* That's when I saw the boat.

It was an old wooden rowboat, stuck in the dark mud at the edge of the water and almost completely hidden by cattails and reeds. Propping my fishing pole against a tree, I made my way carefully over to the boat, concerned with the possibility of stirring up a water snake. As I leaned over the splintery side, peering in at a couple of inches of brown water teeming with mosquito larvae, an idea began to form in my head. I could fix up the boat. Patch any holes it might have and sand it smooth. Maybe even get it to float.

I had learned to float on my back in the swimming pool, but I hadn't been able to enjoy it. I was always afraid that I might accidentally float too far and end up in the deep end where the water was over my head. If I got the boat to float, I could tie it to a tree to keep it close to shore and float in it without even having to get wet.

There were no oars in the boat, just a rusty blue coffee can filled with cement lying in the bottom, a homemade anchor tied to the bow with a hunk of dirty gray rope. Maybe I could use the rope to pull the boat out of the mud, I thought. I hauled out the heavy metal can and, dropping it on the ground, grabbed hold of the rope near the end where it was tied to the boat. Planting my feet firmly, I leaned back with my full weight and pulled. The rope broke almost immediately and my feet flew out from under me, sending me tumbling awkwardly backward into the tall weeds.

The fall knocked the wind out of me and I had to lie there for a few minutes, waiting to catch my breath. After a while, I heard a soft tinkling, like the sound of the wind chimes that hung from the corner of our front porch. Closing my eyes, I listened. It wasn't a bird, that much I could tell. But what could be making the sound? When I stood up, I was shocked to discover that flatlander boy, Pooch, standing a few feet away from me, his hands sunk deep in his pockets. Startled, I screamed— and to my surprise, so did he.

"What are *you* screaming for?" I said, putting my hand over my thudding heart. "You're the one who scared me."

He took his hands out of his pockets and quickly stepped backward.

He was still wearing his long pants and long-sleeved shirt, but for some reason he'd added a red necktie to the outfit. His eyes were small and dark, like two raisins pressed into a ball of soft dough, and now that I was close enough, I could see that his freckled nose was crooked and set slightly off center on his face. I pushed my glasses up with a knuckle and pulled them partway back down.

"Who do you think you are, spying on me like that?" I demanded.

He took another step backward.

"I wasn't spying on you," he said. "Honest."

He looked ridiculous in his necktie.

"Why are you so dressed up?" I asked. "It's summer, in case you haven't noticed. Don't you have any shorts?"

He looked down, nervously fingering his tie. Then he looked back up at me and swallowed a couple of times before answering.

"I don't usually wear a tie," he began. His voice cracked and he swallowed again before continuing. "I put it on for you. I thought maybe I should be dressed up. You know, out of respect."

"What are you talking about?"

"I can take it off if you want," he said quickly. "I wasn't sure what to wear. I've never done this before."

"Done what? Scared someone half to death?"

He broke into a goofy grin.

"You think that's funny?" I snapped. "You could give somebody a heart attack, sneaking up on them like that."

His smile faded immediately.

"I'm—I'm sorry," he stammered. "I didn't mean to scare you. Honest. It's just, well, you have to admit, it is kind of funny, you know, the idea of *me* scaring *you*."

"Yeah. Hilarious," I said sarcastically. "But maybe that's your idea of fun where you come from."

"I'm from the city," he said.

I didn't need to ask him which city he meant, since people from New York City always referred to it as "the city," as if it were the only one worth mentioning.

He stepped forward, extending his hand for me to shake.

"My name is Robert, but you can call me Pooch," he said.

I crossed my arms over my chest, making it clear I had no intention of shaking his hand.

"Don't you city people know it's rude to spy on someone?" I said, even though I'd been spying on him myself earlier.

Pooch let his hand drop down by his side. Then he started scratching his elbow through his shirtsleeve.

"I wasn't spying," he said. "I was waiting."

"For what?"

"For you," he said, still scratching.

"How could you be waiting for me? Nobody even knows I'm here."

"The lady at the post office does," he said. "She's the one who told me."

"Francine? How would she know where I was? She must have been talking about somebody else."

Pooch shook his head.

"She was talking about you. I'm positive."

Flatlanders were such know-it-alls.

"How can you be *positive* she was talking about me? You don't even know who I am," I told him.

"Yes, I do," he said. "You're Tracy Allen. The girl who drowned in the lake."

I was so surprised, my mouth dropped open like the metal flap on the end of a mailbox.

"*Tracy Allen?* How could I be Tracy Allen? Don't you know what *drowned* means?"

"I know what it means," he said.

"Then how could I be her? What do you think I am, a ghost or something?"

"Well," he said, looking up at me, "aren't you?"

I laughed.

"Do I look like a ghost?" I asked.

"All except for the glasses," he said. "I didn't know ghosts wore glasses. And I thought you'd be more see-through. I can't believe I'm standing here talking to you. This is the greatest thing that's ever happened to me."

I didn't know if it was my true nature rearing its ugly head again or if I was justifiably mad because he'd snuck up on me and his mother had thrown a stone at my dog, but whatever the reason, I decided to have a little fun.

"You're right," I told him. "I am the ghost of Tracy Allen."

And he believed me.

CHAPTER NINE

You Can't Be True

"The most fun part about being a ghost is flying and the hardest part is walking through walls—it's not as easy as it looks."

I was perched on a rock, my knees tucked up under my nightgown, and Pooch was sitting on the ground at my feet hanging on every word.

"Do you know any other ghosts?" he asked.

He had taken off his necktie and stuffed it into his back pocket.

"Tons," I told him. "We all get together and have tea parties. Ghosts love tea parties."

"Where are all these other ghosts?" he asked, nervously looking around.

"There are three sitting in that tree over there," I said, pointing. "And don't look now, but there's a big fat one standing right behind you."

He jumped up and spun around, and I had to bite my lip to keep from laughing.

"Where?" he whispered. "I don't see anything,"

"That's 'cause ghosts are invisible, " I told him. "Everybody knows that."

Pooch looked at me and squinched up his eyebrows.

"How come *you're* not invisible?" he asked.

I was having a ball. I'd never met anybody so gullible.

"The reason I'm not invisible is because I'm tired today," I said, faking a big yawn. "Invisibility wears off when you're sleepy."

It felt a little bit like being in a play, except there was only one person in the audience and instead of having to memorize lines, I could make things up as I went along.

"Do you know why ghosts moan?" I asked.

Pooch thought about it for a second. "To scare people?" he said.

"Nope. We moan because we're hungry."

I grabbed my stomach and moaned loudly to demonstrate.

"I've got a granola bar," he said, quickly reaching

into one of his many pockets. "It's a little smushed, but you can have it if you want."

I hadn't had much acting experience. In fact, I had been in a play only once, the year before, in fourth grade. I got nervous when I had to speak in public, but after years of being on the costume committee and painting scenery for our class plays, Annie had convinced me that we ought to try out together for the parts of two Native American sisters in a play our teacher had chosen called *Lenape Drums*. Annie and a tall, dark-haired girl named Danielle ended up being cast as the sisters, and I was given the role of Crow Tongue, the town gossip. It wasn't a big part, but I did have one important scene, where I had to deliver a speech over the deathbed of my husband, who was being played by a boy in my class named Harris Kohler. I can still remember the lines I spoke:

My beloved,
As the moon grows pale and slips from the night sky,
Do not be afraid.
I will find you in the sparrow's song
And in the firefly's light.
Do not be afraid, my beloved.
Your soul will live forever in my heart.

At the dress rehearsal when Harris Kohler lay on the stage supposedly dead and I was about to deliver my big speech, he got a terrible case of the giggles. What set him off was my necklace. My mother had made it out of brightly painted macaroni strung onto one of my father's leather bootlaces. For some reason, the sight of that macaroni got to Harris, and once he started laughing he just couldn't stop. I was so afraid that it would happen during the performance that I became instantly paralyzed with stage fright. I would never have been able to go on if Annie hadn't come to my rescue.

"Don't worry," she told me after the rehearsal. "I'll take care of Harris."

At the performance that night, I delivered my death-bed speech without a hitch, and even though I wore the macaroni necklace, Harris Kohler lay still as a river stone, the crisp new twenty-dollar bill Annie's grand-mother had sent her for her birthday tucked into the front pocket of his pants.

Despite my limited experience on the stage, Pooch seemed to be swallowing my act hook, line, and sinker. He pulled the granola bar out of his pocket and held it out to me.

I shook my head.

"Thanks, but ghosts can't eat granola bars," I told

him. "Everything we eat has to be white—otherwise it shows through. I eat mostly marshmallows and mashed potatoes."

Pooch squinched up his eyebrows again.

"Remember those tea parties you were telling me about?" he said. "Tea isn't white, so how come it doesn't show through when you drink it?"

He was a careful listener, and I was going to have to stay on my toes if I wanted to keep him on the line.

"We call them tea parties, but we don't actually drink tea," I explained. "We have hot water with lemon instead. Or sometimes hot milk."

"I can't drink milk," said Pooch, folding his arms and scratching both elbows at the same time. "I'm lactose intolerant. I'm also allergic to feather pillows, dust mites, pollen, bee stings, walnuts, and—"

"Is there anything you're not allergic to?" I interrupted.

"Sugarless gum," he said, reaching into the pocket of his shirt. "Want a piece?"

I did, but I shook my head when he held out the package to me. I wasn't sure whether gum counted as a see-through food or not. Pooch unwrapped a stick of pink gum and folded it into his mouth.

"Do you think any of your ghost friends would like

a piece?" he asked, waving the pack in the air.

I'd forgotten I'd told him there were other ghosts.

"They all left," I said. "There's a big tea party over in Washerville today. I'm the only one here now."

Pooch blew a little pink bubble, which popped and stuck to his lips. He grinned that goofy grin again, and this time I noticed there were gaps where some of his permanent teeth hadn't grown in yet.

"How old are you?" I asked him.

"Nine," he answered, picking at the remnants of bubble sticking to his lower lip. "Same as you."

I was eleven and a half. Even though I'd started school a year later than everybody else, making me the oldest in my class, I was used to people assuming I was younger than I really was because I was so small for my age.

"I figured that's how it worked," he went on. "However old you are when you die, that's how old you stay forever, right?"

Now I understood. He thought I was nine because Tracy Allen had been nine when she drowned.

"Is it true what they say about the light?" asked Pooch.

"What light?" I asked.

"The white light you see right before you die."

I shivered. It was one thing to make up stories about ghosts having tea parties and walking through walls, but I didn't want to have to think about how Tracy Allen must have felt when she drowned, or the last thing she saw before she died.

"Aren't you hot in those clothes?" I asked, changing the subject.

"Yeah, but I have to keep covered up because I burn easily," Pooch explained.

"Ever heard of sunscreen?" I asked.

"I'm allergic to PABA."

"What's PABA?"

"I'm not sure," he said. "But whatever it is, I'm allergic to it."

He wasn't exactly what I had expected. There was something sad about him, standing there talking about his allergies with the end of his necktie hanging out of his pocket like a little red tail.

"Where'd you get that nickname of yours, anyway?" I asked.

Pooch lifted his foot and used the toe of his shoe to scratch the back of his leg.

"Richard the Third came up with it."

"Richard the Third?"

"My mom had three boyfriends in a row named Richard," Pooch explained.

I must have looked surprised, because he added, "My parents got divorced a long time ago. My mom does internet dating."

"Oh," I said, having a hard time imagining what it would feel like to have a mom who went out on dates with someone other than your dad.

Pooch bent down and scratched his knee.

"You sure are itchy," I said. "You got bug bites or something?"

Pooch shook his head.

"Eczema. It gets worse when I'm nervous."

"Am I making you nervous?" I asked.

"No, no," he said quickly, but then he blushed. "Well, maybe a little."

We were both quiet for a minute.

"Anyway, I got the name on account of the scratching," Pooch told me. "Richard the Third said I looked like a dog with fleas. He started calling me Pooch and it stuck. I have some lotion at home that helps, but I forgot to bring it."

There was another silence between us. Pooch slipped his hands into his front pockets and began to jiggle them. To my surprise, the air suddenly filled with a familiar tinkling sound.

"Oh," I said, "so that was you before. What have you got in there?"

CHAPTER TEN

Ting-a-Ling-a-Jingle

"Bottles," answered Pooch, giving his pockets another jiggle.

"What kind of bottles?"

"Little ones," he said. "They used to have booze in them, but they don't anymore."

My parents didn't drink, not even beer, and they didn't smoke either. Now that I understood the damage that Grace's drinking had done to me, I was even more aware of what an evil thing alcohol could be.

"Do you drink booze?" I asked warily.

"Of course not!" He laughed. "Our next-door neighbor in the city is a flight attendant. She brings me empty bottles sometimes because she knows I like to collect stuff."

I felt a glimmer of hope inside. Was it possible

this flatlander boy and I actually had something in common?

"What do you like to collect?" I asked.

Pooch reached into his pocket and pulled out a clear glass bottle with a red metal screw top. The label had been scratched off so it was easy to see inside.

"Check out this gold bug," he said handing me the bottle. "Did you know that if you paint yourself gold, your skin won't be able to breathe and you'll suffocate to death? I saw that in a movie once."

I peered in at the insect crawling around on the bottom of Pooch's bottle. I knew what it was because my mother waged a daily war against them during the summer, carrying a table knife and a cup of soapy water out to her garden so she could knock them off of the bushes into the cup and drown them.

"That's a Japanese beetle," I said.

"Japanese, huh? Are they rare?" asked Pooch.

"Maybe in New York City," I told him.

He pulled out another bottle and held it up for me to see.

"I found this out in the ditch by the road. It's some kind of baby lizard. Good thing Komodo dragons don't live around here. They're the heaviest lizards on earth—and their mouths are so full of bacteria, if they bite you you'll die of gangrene."

No wonder his mother had called him Doctor Doom. He sure knew a lot of things that could kill you.

"That's a newt," I said, pointing at the yellow-bellied salamander in the bottle. "And don't worry, it won't bite you—it doesn't even have teeth."

"How big do newts get?" he asked.

I held my thumb and forefinger about three inches apart to show him. "But if you leave it in that bottle much longer, it's going to dry out and shrivel up to the size of a toothpick," I said. "And it'll stink to high heaven too."

Pooch quickly unscrewed the top, squatted down, and shook the newt out of the bottle onto the ground. We both watched it crawl off.

"What else have you got?" I asked.

He lifted his foot and scratched the back of his leg with the top of his shoe again.

"Well, there is one more thing," he said. "At least I *think* there is."

Pooch reached into his pocket, slowly took out a bottle, and held it up for me to see. There was nothing in it.

"Is this supposed to be a joke?" I asked.

"Don't you see it?"

"See what?" I took the bottle from him and held it up close to my face. "There's nothing in here."

I started to untwist the cap.

"Don't let it out!" cried Pooch.

I stopped midtwist.

"Let what out?" I looked again at the empty bottle.

"It's a mouse," he said.

There was no way he could have fit a mouse into that bottle. The neck was as narrow as my little finger.

"Was it a baby mouse?" I asked him.

"Nope. Regular sized. I found it in a trap right before I came down here."

"You mean it was *dead*?"

"Not quite," he said. "My mom saw mouse droppings on the kitchen counter when we got here, so she set some old traps we found under the sink. She used peanut butter for bait. If a mouse tries to eat it, the trap snaps closed and breaks its neck. See, there's this little spring and when the mouse steps on the—"

"I know how a mousetrap works," I interrupted impatiently. "What I don't know is why you'd try to catch a mouse in a bottle if you'd already caught it in a trap."

"The traps only catch their bodies," said Pooch.

"What else is there?"

He gave me a strange look.

"That's a pretty funny question coming from you," he said.

It took a minute before I realized what he was trying to say, and then the hair on my arms prickled up.

"I read somewhere that your soul leaves your body when you breathe out for the last time," said Pooch. "I could tell the mouse was about to die, so I put the bottle up against its nose to see if I could catch its soul on the way out."

"That's creepy," I told him.

"Why?" he said. "Death is a natural thing, just like getting born."

"Death is the opposite of getting born," I said.

"They're both natural," Pooch insisted. "And interesting. Especially death."

"I don't see what's so interesting about it," I told him.

"That's because you already know all the answers."

"What answers?" I asked.

"Well, for starters, what's the deal with reincarnation? And what about heaven? If you don't believe in heaven while you're alive, and then you die and find out you were wrong—can you still go there?"

My head was beginning to spin. I'd gone to church with my parents plenty of Sundays, but I never really listened when Reverend Fyfe delivered his sermons. He used too many big words, and his deep rumbling voice made me feel sleepy. I had no idea what the rules were about getting into heaven, let alone reincarnation. I was beginning to wonder if I'd bitten off more than I could chew with this whole pretending-to-be-a-ghost thing.

"Look," I said, handing the empty bottle back to Pooch, "I think there's something we'd better get straight here. Ghosts don't like to talk about death."

"Really?" he said. I could tell he was disappointed.

"There must be other things you're interested in."

He thought for a minute.

"Dinosaurs."

Not a favorite subject of mine.

"Anything else?"

"I like to build stuff," he said. "I'm pretty good at it too. I made the Empire State Building out of marshmallows and toothpicks once. Too bad I don't have it anymore—you could eat it for dinner. At least the marshmallow part."

At the mention of food, my stomach grumbled. That peanut butter and grape jelly sandwich I'd eaten earlier was beginning to wear off. However, my concern about the rumbling in my stomach was overshadowed by my excitement about what Pooch had just revealed.

"If you're good at building things, does that mean you're good at fixing things too?" I asked.

"I guess so."

"If I show you something, do you promise not to tell anybody?" I said.

Pooch used his index finger to draw a little X over the pocket of his shirt.

"Cross my heart and hope to die," he said.

The words were barely out when he clapped his hand over his mouth.

"Sorry," he told me. "I didn't mean to say that part about dying."

I had to laugh. He had the exact same guilty look on his face that Jack always got when we caught him sleeping on the couch or eating cat food out of Honey's dish.

"Don't worry. That doesn't count," I told Pooch. "It's just an expression."

Pooch looked relieved.

"All I was trying to say was that I won't tell any-body," he said. "I'm good at keeping secrets."

"In that case," I told him, "follow me."

And I led him into the tall weeds.

CHAPTER ELEVEN

Little Boat

Pooch gave a low whistle of appreciation when he saw the boat.

"Is it yours?" he asked, resting his hands on the side.

"You know what they say. Finders keepers . . ."

"Losers weepers," he said, finishing the thought.

We were interrupted by a commotion in some nearby bushes. A few seconds later a rabbit came shooting out into the open, followed by Jack in hot pursuit, his tongue hanging out of the side of his mouth.

"Look at him go!" Pooch shouted.

They rounded a curve, but just as Jack was closing in, the rabbit zigged, then zagged, then bolted back into the bushes. Jack skidded to a stop, lost his balance, and fell over onto his hip. By the time he'd struggled back to his feet, the rabbit was long gone. Jack stood staring after it, panting hard.

"Did you see that?" cried Pooch, "He came *this* close to catching that thing."

"Trust me, the only thing Jack ever catches is a face full of skunk squirt," I said.

Pooch's eyebrows bunched up.

"Does he belong to you?" he asked. "Because I'm pretty sure I've seen that dog before."

I'd forgotten that Pooch and Jack had already met.

"He's not mine," I said, figuring it would be easier to deny it than to have to explain how a ghost could have a pet. "The only reason I know his name is because he belongs to someone who lives around here and I hear them calling him sometimes."

"Oh," said Pooch. "Do you know what happened to his leg?"

"He probably got hit by a car," I told him.

Pooch stood with his left arm bent behind his back in order to use his thumb to scratch between his shoulder blades. Together we watched Jack wade out into the lake until he was chest deep and noisily lapping up water with his long tongue. Pooch kicked at a clump of old cattails, setting loose a shower of pale fluff.

"Can I ask you something?" he said.

"That depends," I told him, hoping I wasn't going

to have to remind him that the subject of death was off limits.

"Do you think if we pull this boat out of the mud, we could fix it up and get it to float?"

We gave it everything we had, but pulling the boat out of the mud proved to be much harder than either of us had anticipated.

"Maybe we should try pushing it instead," Pooch suggested.

I wasn't wild about the idea of wading out into the water.

"Ghosts aren't supposed to get wet," I told him. "We wrinkle."

Pooch didn't question me; he just sat down and began taking off his shoes and socks. Then he rolled up his pant legs and waded out into the water.

"Brrr!" he cried, wrapping his arms around himself and hopping up and down. "It's freezing!" But I could tell he didn't really mind it.

I pulled while Pooch pushed, but even working at it from both ends our combined efforts were not enough to budge the boat. After a while Pooch waded back out and leaned over the side of the boat, looking in at the stagnant water pooled in the bottom.

"It wouldn't be so heavy if it didn't have all this water in it," he said.

"We could bail it out," I suggested. "All we need is an empty can."

I thought of the tin can I'd left behind in the flower bed at home, where I'd been interrupted digging for worms. If only I'd remembered to bring it along. We kicked around in the weeds for a while hoping to find something we could use, but the only thing we turned up were a few moldy candy wrappers.

"How about we use a couple of my bottles?" Pooch offered.

But after five minutes of painstakingly filling and emptying the tiny bottles, we abandoned that idea in favor of a different approach. Taking up positions on either side, we began to rock the boat like a giant cradle between us, finally succeeding in loosening it enough to be able to flip it over. Jack sniffed at the dark water with great interest as it ran out onto the ground and quickly soaked in.

"He loves anything that smells bad," I explained.

"Same with Dixie," said Pooch.

"Who's Dixie?" I asked, suddenly remembering the

anxious concern in Pooch's mother's voice when she'd asked where Dixie was.

"Dixie's my mom's dog," he said. "She's named after a paper cup."

"What kind is she?" I asked.

"Maltese. She's purebred, but she looks like a dirty old bathmat. And she bites. Especially me."

"How come you're allergic to all those other things, but you're not allergic to dogs?"

"I am," Pooch said. "Unfortunately, Dixie's hypo-allergenic."

Without the water in it, the boat, although still heavy, was light enough for us to be able to drag it up onto dry ground. My heart was pounding so hard from the effort, I could feel it in my cheeks. I sat down on the ground to catch my breath, and Pooch, who was also winded, bent over, resting his hands on his knees. He reached around and started scratching the back of his neck.

"You nervous again?" I asked.

"Actually, yeah. See, there's something I think I'd better tell you," he said. "It's about where my mom and I are staying."

"I know where you're staying," I told him.

His eyes widened.

"You do?"

I nodded.

"I also know that your mom doesn't like the house very much. Or Clydesdale. Or three-legged dogs either."

Pooch's cheeks turned pink again.

"She's not usually mean. She was just in a bad mood because her face was hurting."

"What's the matter with her face?"

"Nothing. But she decided she didn't like it anymore, so she got it fixed," he said.

"What do you mean, fixed?"

Pooch put his hands on his cheeks and pulled the skin taut. "Plastic surgery," he told me through his stretched lips. "She'd kill me if she knew I was talking about it. We came up here so nobody would know. It takes a couple of weeks for the swelling to go down."

I thought about the floppy hat, the jewelry, and the big dark glasses.

"Is your mom a movie star or something?" I asked.

Pooch laughed. "No. She works in a bank. But she wants to get married again, and she says men don't like women who look their age."

"How old is she?" I asked.

"Thirty-eight."

I thought about my mother's smooth, wide face. She didn't have any wrinkles and she would be fifty on her next birthday.

"Where's your dad?" I asked.

"East Eighty-first Street. I see him on Wednesdays. We have dinner. His girlfriend is a Pilates instructor. The first time I met her, she told me that exercise is her life."

Now I had to try to imagine what it would feel like to have a father who had a girlfriend.

"Do you mind?" Pooch asked.

"Mind what?" I said.

"That we're staying in your house. I mean, it must be kind of weird knowing some kid you don't even know is sleeping in your room."

I'd never been inside the Allen house, but I'd always wondered what it was like. I imagined that the air was cold and damp and that it was filled with a sad, musty kind of smell. Houses have a way of soaking up the lives of the people who live inside them.

"How do you know it's my room?" I asked.

"You scratched your initials on the windowsill, remember?" said Pooch. "T.A." He drew the letters in the air.

A shiver ran up my spine. I didn't even know what Tracy Allen looked like, but she suddenly seemed more real to me than ever before.

"I don't mind that you're staying at my house," I told Pooch. "It's not like I live there anymore."

"Where *do* you live?" he asked.

"That subject is off limits too. No personal questions allowed."

Jack waded out of the water and shook himself so hard he fell over. Then he rolled onto his back and lay in the dirt, belly up, to dry. My stomach grumbled again, this time in earnest.

"I'm kind of hungry," I said.

Pooch's face lit up.

"Why don't you come over for dinner?" he suggested. "I don't think we have any marshmallows in the house, but we definitely have milk. And maybe my mom could make you some mashed potatoes."

He was all excited about the idea of my coming over, but as hungry as I happened to be and as curious as I was to see the inside of the Allen house, there was no way I was going to go over there in a ripped-up nightgown, pretending to be a ghost in front of Pooch's mother.

"Maybe some other time," I said.

But Pooch persisted.

"We don't have to tell my mom who you are if that's the problem. We could just say you're a neighbor girl or something."

I couldn't tell him why that was funny, or that what I really wanted for dinner was pork chops with apple cider gravy, since clearly that wasn't on the white-food list.

"Thanks," I said. "But I need to get going."

Pooch started scratching the back of his neck.

"What's the matter now?" I said.

"Are you going to come back tomorrow?" he asked me.

"Of course I am. It's my boat, remember? You think I'm just going to walk away and let you have all the fun of fixing it up? I'll bring some rope—that way we can tie the boat to a tree and it won't float away."

Pooch was looking at me funny; his eyes narrowed to slits and his head tilted to the side.

"You're not lying, are you?" he said.

The sun, which had momentarily slipped behind a cloud, reemerged, spilling its yolky glow over us.

"Lying about what?" I said.

"About coming back tomorrow."

I breathed a silent sigh of relief. I knew it wasn't nice of me to be leading Pooch on, but if he figured out

I'd been lying to him, he might get mad, and then he wouldn't want to help with the boat.

"You worry too much," I told him. "I said I was coming back, didn't I?"

"Honest?" said Pooch.

His round little face was so full of hope, it almost hurt to look at it.

"Honest," I told him. "I'll meet you back here at ten o'clock tomorrow morning. Now cover your eyes and count to a hundred. Don't try to follow me and don't tell anyone you saw me down here either. Not even your mom."

Pooch drew an X over his heart with his finger. Then he covered his eyes, and I left him counting by the lake.

CHAPTER TWELVE

Round and Round

"If you don't believe in heaven while you're alive, but then when you die you find out it's actually a real place, can you still go there?"

I was sitting at the kitchen table, finishing up my breakfast. My mother was standing at the sink, stringing beans.

"Where in the world did that question come from?" she asked.

"Nowhere," I said. "I was just wondering. Is that where Grandpa Colty is? Heaven?"

My mother looked at me.

"Your grandpa Colty was a very good man. If there is a heaven, I'm sure that's where he is."

"Where else could he be?" I asked.

"Different people believe different things," she said, turning her attention back to the beans.

"What do *you* believe?" I asked.

"Well, if I had to put it into words, I guess I'd say that I believe life is like a big circle," she said. "Each ending marks a new beginning."

"Some people believe that your soul leaves your body the last time you breathe out," I said, remembering what Pooch had told me.

My mother set down her knife.

"It's a beautiful day outside; we don't need to be talking about last breaths, do we?"

I shrugged and took a bite of my pink eggs.

Pink eggs had been a favorite of mine when I was little. You make them by frying an egg and then at the last minute putting a drop of water in the pan and covering it up to steam the yolk until it turns pink. I hadn't had them in years, but my mother had made them for me that morning without asking.

"I just thought it was interesting, that's all," I said.

My mother's face suddenly brightened.

"Speaking of interesting, I have some interesting news," she said. "Guess what—we have a new neighbor. Someone has rented the Allen house."

I almost choked, but I took a swallow of milk to cover it. I wasn't in the habit of lying to my mother, but I didn't want her to know that I already knew about the new neighbors. It would only lead to questions. She'd noticed my torn nightgown, of course, but she'd been satisfied with the explanation I'd given her about going for a long walk with Jack the day before and having caught it on some blackberry brambles.

"It's a woman and her little boy," my mother went on. "Francine told me about them this morning when I went down to get the mail."

"Oh," I said, trying to keep my voice even as I peeled a piece of crust off my bread and laid it along the edge of the plate. "What did she say about them?"

My mother hesitated, obviously weighing whether or not to repeat what she'd heard.

"You know how Francine likes to talk," she said with a wave of her hand.

"What did she say?" I asked, doing my best not to sound overly interested.

"Apparently the woman wasn't feeling well, because she stayed out in the car. Only the boy came inside. Francine said he was odd—scratching himself a lot and asking all kinds of strange questions."

"Francine should keep her big trap shut," I said, surprised at the feeling with which the words came out.

"*Verbie,*" my mother scolded, "that's no way to talk."

"Francine's the one who's saying things she shouldn't.

102

What's wrong with asking questions? And what's so odd about being itchy? Everybody gets itchy sometimes. Maybe he's got a rash, or an allergy or something. Did you ever think of that?"

My mother was staring at me.

"What's gotten into you?" she asked.

"What's gotten into *you*?" I said, pushing back my chair with such force it fell over backward. I righted the chair and carried my dishes over to the sink to rinse them off. All I wanted was to get out of there before I did something worse than knock over my chair.

"Let's not end on a bad note," my mother said, taking the wet plate from me and putting it in the dishwasher. "We were having such a nice talk before."

"We were?" I said.

"You and I have always been like two peas in a pod, Verbie."

Two peas in a pod? I could barely stand to be around her anymore. I knew who I was really like.

"If you say so," I said as I swirled water around in my glass before pouring it down the drain and handing the glass to her.

"What are your plans this morning?" she asked in a tone I recognized as the same cautious voice she always used when she reached out her hand to a dog she wasn't sure was safe to pet. Maybe I wasn't the only one who saw the similarities between Teddy and myself.

"I could use some help getting the strawberries ready for the shortcakes," my mother told me. "I'm going to be making two this year—one for the raffle and one for us. Won't that be nice?"

"I've already got plans," I said.

"You do?" She sounded pleased.

"I'm going for a walk."

"Oh," she said, clearly disappointed. "Another walk?"

Down at the lake with Pooch the day before, pulling the boat out of the mud, I'd felt happier than I'd been in a long time. Pooch was a nine-year-old flatlander, an itchy boy who believed in ghosts and didn't know beans about bugs or salamanders, but I didn't care. I liked being with him. He didn't know who I really was, and when I was with him I got to pretend that I didn't know either.

I hadn't thought about Teddy or Grace or Mike Colter even once when I was with Pooch, and I hadn't missed Annie either, but a ten-minute conversation with my mother was all it took to tie me up in knots again.

"One day you're telling me I ought to go out and get some fresh air, and the next day you act like there's something wrong with going for a walk!" I shouted at her. "Make up your mind, will you?"

My mother sighed, and dried her hands on the dish towel hanging from the refrigerator door handle.

"I didn't mean to step on your toes or imply there was anything wrong with taking a walk. Just do me a favor and get dressed before you go outside today, okay? That nightie is a disgrace. If the new neighbors see you walking around looking like that, they're going to think I'm the worst mother on earth."

"Maybe you are."

I should have gotten out of there sooner, before things had escalated to the point where I couldn't control my own tongue. Those three ugly words hung in the air between us like black smoke until finally my mother spoke.

"Have a nice walk, Verbena," she said. Then she turned her back, opened the faucet, and began to rinse the beans.

I left my mother in the kitchen and went into the bathroom to splash cold water on my face. I felt awful.

"Who are you?" I thought as I stared at myself in the medicine cabinet mirror.

I hadn't meant what I'd said. As annoyed as I got with my mother sometimes, I knew I was lucky to have her. If she and my father hadn't taken me, there's no telling what might have happened to me. Still, I couldn't bring myself to go back into the kitchen and apologize to my mother. I couldn't bear to see the hurt look on her face. Even though she had to have known the day would come when her perfect little girl would show her true colors, I still felt guilty about disappointing her.

Pooch would be heading down to the lake soon, and I was dying to leave my troubles behind and get back to the boat. I'd come up with a list of supplies we would need—sandpaper, glue, a hammer, and a few other odds and ends I thought we could use. My father had all those things out in his workshop, but I wasn't allowed to go in there when he wasn't around. Besides, he wouldn't have let me take any tools away with me. He was very particular about his things.

The floor of the shop was always swept clean, the wood scraps piled neatly by the door. Over his workbench the wall was made of pegboard, the outline of every tool he owned drawn around it in black Magic Marker so that he'd know exactly where to put it back after he'd finished using it. A row of hammers marched across the wall like steadfast soldiers, shoulders squared, heads all facing in the same direction. Screwdrivers with translucent red handles were arranged in descending order of size like a family posing for a formal portrait.

The whole place smelled of sawdust and varnish, and there was a feeling of peace and purposefulness in the air that reminded me for some reason of church.

There was a closet off the mudroom in the back of the house where my father kept a stash of old tools for quick fix-it jobs around the house. I decided to look there for what I needed. On my way down the hall, I passed a wall of family photographs and accidentally brushed up against one of the wooden frames with my shoulder, knocking it crooked on the hook. I paused to straighten it.

It was a picture of the two Colter brothers standing on the front steps of the house. There were enough similarities between them that you could tell they were related, but it was obvious just from the photo that their personalities were completely different. My father, Tom, in jeans and a flannel shirt, smiled directly into the camera, his arm draped loosely around his younger brother's shoulders. Mike held his arms straight down by his sides, and he was looking away from the camera, scowling. He wore a leather jacket and sunglasses, and his hair was all slicked down with grease and combed back like the guys who hung around the Washerville Gas and Go at night. That photograph had interested me long before I found out that I was Mike Colter's daughter.

"How come Daddy and Uncle Mike don't match?" I remember asking my mother one day.

We were sitting together on the front porch in the wooden chair swing my grandfather had hung there years ago for my grandma Betsy when they had lived in the house. My mother pushed herself up out of the swing, took me by the hand, and led me over to the edge of the yard where a tangle of blackberry brambles grew.

"Look here, Verbie," she said. "See how some of the berries on this bush are plump and juicy?" She reached out and barely touched a ripe berry, which was all it took to separate it from its nub. It rolled into her open palm and she held it out to me. "You can tell just by looking at it how sweet this one will taste."

I took the berry from her and slipped it into my mouth. It was soft and full of juice. "Now look at these other berries," she said. "They're growing right alongside the sweet ones on the very same bush, but for some reason they turned out small and bitter, like hard little fists full of seeds." She touched a small, dark purple berry with her fingertip, but it held tightly to its nub.

"Those are the Uncle Mikes, aren't they?" I said.

My mother put her arm around me, resting her cheek on the top of my head.

"Everybody was put here on this earth for a reason, Sugarpea," she said. "Even Mike Colter."

"Was he really as bad as everybody says he was?" I asked.

"Yes," she said. "But there must have been a little bit of good in him too—otherwise—"

She never finished that sentence, but years later standing in the hallway looking at the photograph of the two Colter brothers, I knew that the reason my mother had stopped herself was because the rest of the sentence probably would have been something like "—otherwise he couldn't have made someone as perfect as you." She hadn't wanted me to know the truth. And she hadn't wanted anybody else to know either. People in small towns don't forget easily. And they don't forgive either. They would have heard the time bomb ticking away inside me and known that trouble was coming.

CHAPTER THIRTEEN

C'mon Back

Pooch was already there when I got to the lake, squatting down in the weeds beside the boat. He didn't see me at first.

"Do you have any idea how ridiculous you look in that?" I called out to him.

He was wearing his mother's big floppy hat. The one I had seen her in the day before.

"It keeps the sun off my face," he called back. "Come look at what I found. It's a hole."

I pushed up my glasses with a knuckle and put one hand over my eyes to shield them from the sun.

"How big is it?"

"Like so," he said, making a circle with his hand about the size of a golf ball to show me. "Come look."

I laid the tools and other supplies down in the grass

and walked over to the boat.

"Is this the only one you found, or are there others?" I asked, squatting down next to Pooch and pressing my fingertips into the ragged opening.

Pooch explained that he'd examined the whole boat and this was the only hole he'd found.

"I was thinking maybe we could plug it up with one of those rubber thingies you use in the bathtub."

"The wood around the hole is rotten," I pointed out. "A plug wouldn't work. The water would leak in around it. What we need is a patch to glue over the hole."

"Do we have a patch?" asked Pooch.

"No," I said, "and we don't have any glue either."

Glue had been one of the things on my list, but the bottle I'd found in the tool closet had been all dried up.

"Hey!" said Pooch, snapping his fingers. "I just thought of something. Why don't we use birch bark and pine gum to patch the hole like the Lenape Indians did with their canoes? I learned all about that last year in school."

Pooch's school must have had the same social studies curriculum as ours, because we'd studied the art of canoe making in fourth grade too. I loved the idea of trying to patch the boat with bark, and it just so happened there was a stand of white birch trees not ten feet away from where we were.

"We can use the hammer claw to peel off the bark. And I brought some nails too," I said. "There are tons of pine trees around here. We can make holes with the nails to get the pitch out."

Pooch squinched up his eyebrows, signaling an oncoming question I had anticipated he might ask.

"Where did you get all that stuff anyway?"

I told him that because I'd slept well the night before, I'd been able to store up enough energy to go invisible and float into somebody's toolshed to borrow a few things.

"It must feel amazing to be invisible," Pooch said wistfully.

"Actually, it tickles," I told him. "Now grab that hammer and let's get started."

I carried the hammer, Pooch followed along behind me in his ridiculous hat, and Jack, who had tagged along again, brought up the rear.

"How does it work?" Pooch asked as we made our

way over to the stand of birch trees. "When you're invisible and you're holding something, does it get invisible too? Or is it like in the movies when they use wires to make it look like things are floating around all by themselves?"

I didn't feel like having to make up answers to Pooch's questions all day. I just wanted to work on the boat.

"No more questions about ghost stuff today, okay?"

Pooch nodded. Then he leaned down to give Jack a pat on the head and immediately sneezed.

"I guess Jack's not hypoallergenic, huh?" I said.

"Correct," said Pooch, pinching his nose to stifle another sneeze.

I chose a birch tree I thought looked good, and slipping the metal claw of the hammer under a piece of loose bark, I tried to ease it away from the trunk. After three or four unsuccessful attempts, I kicked the tree in frustration. No matter how careful I was, the papery bark kept splitting into narrow strips, like the curls of bread crust I'd left on the edge of my plate at breakfast.

"How in the world did the Indians *do* this?" I said, pausing to wipe my sweaty hands on my nightgown.

"You're not supposed to call them *Indians* any-more," Pooch told me. "You're supposed to say *Native Americans*."

"That's only in school," I said. "In real life everyone still says Indian."

After a few more attempts to pull off a piece of bark big enough to use as a patch, I lowered the hammer again. My arms ached and a tight knot had formed between my shoulder blades.

"This isn't working," I said.

"I can take a turn if you want," Pooch offered.

His arms were even skinnier than mine, but I handed over the hammer anyway. I'd pretty much massacred the bark on the tree I'd been working on, so we moved a little deeper into the grove and chose a fresh trunk.

"If you were an Indian, what do you think your name would be?" Pooch asked as he chose his starting point and carefully worked the hammer claw under the papery white skin of the tree. "You know, like Running Bear or Sitting Squaw."

"I don't know," I said. "What about you?"

"With my luck, if I was an Indian, one of my mother's boyfriends would get to pick my name," he said.

I laughed.

"I'd probably get stuck with a name as weird as the

one I have now," I told him.

I didn't realize my mistake until it was too late.

"What's so weird about the name Tracy?" Pooch asked.

The answer, of course, was nothing. I was thinking of my own name, Verbena. I'd been so busy trying to peel bark, I'd forgotten I was supposed to be pretending to be Tracy Allen.

"Tracy is actually my middle name," I said, frantically trying to cover my tracks. "But don't ask me what my real name is because I never tell anybody."

"What letter does it start with. Maybe I can guess," said Pooch.

"No," I told him, "I don't want you to guess. Let's just get the bark off the tree so we can patch the boat, okay?"

It turned out that Pooch had a way with birch bark. On his first try he successfully pulled off a piece more than big enough for our patching purposes.

"Now all we need is some pitch," I said.

We went back and got the nails, which Pooch put into one of his many pockets. His pants were a different color but they were the same kind as the ones he'd had on the day before.

"Is that the only kind of pants you ever wear?" I asked.

"Pretty much," said Pooch. "I need a lot of pockets."

"What for?"

"All kinds of stuff." Pooch started patting his pockets. "I've got tissues, hand sanitizer, my bottles in case I find anything cool, and my EpiPen, of course."

"What's that?"

"It's got medicine in it in case I have an allergy attack, like if a bee stings me."

"I don't like bees," I said.

"Me neither," said Pooch.

We quickly discovered that it wasn't necessary to make holes in a pine tree in order to get pitch; beads of amber gum oozed out of the bark without any help from us. We used the nails to scrape the pitch directly onto the patch.

"Man, is this stuff sticky," said Pooch. "I sure hope I'm not allergic to it, 'cause it's getting all over me."

"How do you know if you're allergic to something—do you start sneezing?" I asked.

"Sometimes. Or sometimes I get hives. If it's really bad my tongue swells up and I can't breathe. You can die from an allergic reaction, but I guess you don't want to hear about that."

"How's your tongue feel right now?" I asked.

Pooch stuck out his tongue and looked down his nose at it.

"So far so good," he said.

It had been almost two years since I had studied the art of canoe making, but the details were still fresh in Pooch's mind.

"The Indians had two ways of storing their canoes to keep them from drying out," he told me. "Either they turned them upside down and put them in the shade under buffalo hides or they filled them up with heavy rocks and sank them in the river until it was time to use them."

"I don't think we need to worry about the boat drying out," I said. "It's still pretty wet from having had all that water in it."

"Good point," said Pooch.

We carried the sticky patch back over to the boat and pressed it onto the side to cover the hole. To our delight, it worked perfectly.

"How long do you think it'll take before it's dry?" Pooch asked as he stood back to admire our handiwork.

"I don't know," I said. "Maybe overnight. As long as it doesn't rain."

Leaving the patch to cure, we turned our attention

to another task, sanding.

"Let's do the seats first," said Pooch, taking a sheet of sandpaper and folding it into a square, "so we won't get splinters when we sit down in her."

I laughed.

"That sounds funny—sit down in *her.*"

"Well, that's what you're supposed to say, isn't it?" said Pooch. "All boats are shes. Come on, help me turn her back over."

Being careful not to dislodge the freshly applied patch, the two of us turned the boat over. When we were done, Pooch hopped in.

"This is awesome!" he cried. "I can't wait 'til tomorrow, when we can see if she floats."

I hiked up my nightgown and was about to climb into the boat to join him when I noticed something. On the side, near the front, was the faint outline of a letter.

"Look," I said.

"What is it?" asked Pooch, clambering out of the boat.

"She has a name."

CHAPTER FOURTEEN

Missing You

"Brittany. Bethany. Beatrice. Beulah."

"Beulah?" I said. "Who would name a boat Beulah?"

"I don't know. I'm just trying to come up with all the *B* names I can think of," said Pooch. "I have an aunt named Beulah."

"If only we had a couple more letters, I bet we could figure it out," I said.

But the *B* was all that remained of the name—the other letters were all long gone.

"We don't even know for sure if it's a girl's name," said Pooch.

"You said yourself all boats are shes."

"Titanic's not a girl's name. It's not even a boy's name. Maybe the *B* stands for something random like Banana or Bubble Wrap."

"What's the point of even trying to guess?" I said.

"We're never going to know for sure."

"Think like an Indian," said Pooch. "You'll feel better."

"What's that supposed to mean?"

"Indians used to choose a name when a person was born and then change the name whenever anything important happened to them. This boat would have just rotted away if you hadn't found it, right? So it doesn't matter what the old name was, because it needs a new name anyway to celebrate having been found."

"Do you know as much about dinosaurs as you know about Indians?" I asked.

"Actually, more," said Pooch.

We spent the rest of that afternoon sanding the boat and trying to come up with a name for it.

"How about Tippy?" Pooch said. "That would be a good name for a boat, don't you think?"

"Are you kidding? That's a terrible name. Who wants a tippy boat?"

"What about Tofu?" Pooch suggested.

"*Tofu?*"

"It's bean curd."

"I know what it is," I said. "I've seen it floating

around in a bucket at the health food store."

"Exactly," said Pooch. "*It floats*. That's why it'd be a great name. Plus it's good for you."

"Spinach is good for you too. Do you think we should name the boat Spinach?" I said.

"Does being dead make everybody grumpy, or were you like this before you were a ghost?"

I stuck my tongue out at Pooch, and he laughed.

I didn't like Tofu or any of the other names Pooch came up with for the boat, and he wasn't wild about any of my names either.

"What do you think about Bonners Darling?" I said.

"Gross," said Pooch.

"Silver Slipper?"

"Even worse."

We finally agreed that each of us would come up with a list of ten possible names for the boat that night, and in the morning we'd meet and compare lists.

"Tomorrow is the Fourth of July, you know," said Pooch.

"I know," I said, refolding the piece of sandpaper I'd been using in order to find a rougher side.

"Do you like fireworks?" he asked. "My mom says

they're going to have some in town. And there's a concert too."

"I used to like fireworks," I said, "but I don't anymore."

"I love them," said Pooch. "I hope it doesn't rain. You can't have fireworks if it rains."

"Is it supposed to rain tomorrow?" I asked.

"They said so on the radio."

"Yeah, well they said that about today too," I said, squinting up at the sky.

The sun was shining brightly, and even though he was wearing the floppy hat, Pooch's nose was beginning to turn pink. I pushed my glasses up with a bent knuckle and pulled them partway back down again.

"Why do you do that?" asked Pooch, who had taken a break from his sanding and was watching me.

"Do what?" I asked.

"Push your glasses up and then pull them back down."

"I don't know," I told him. "It's just something I do."

"Can you see without your glasses on?" he asked.

"Not very well."

"That's what I figured. Otherwise why would you wear them, right? Hey, maybe you were a bat in a past life and that's why you can't see."

"Thanks a lot," I said. "Bats are hideous mice with wings. And they eat bugs."

"I think mice are cute," said Pooch.

"You would. What did you do with that mouse that you caught in the mousetrap?" I asked.

"My mom picked it up with some salad tongs and put it the trash," he told me.

With all the unfortunate pets my mother had taken in over the years, there had been plenty of deaths. Sometimes my mother would take the bodies back to Dr. Finn at the shelter, but the smaller animals she quietly buried in our backyard. My mother would never have put any animal, even a mouse, in the trash.

"When I die, I want to be cremated and have my ashes sprinkled outside Gray's Papaya," Pooch said.

"Where's that?" I asked.

"It's on the corner of Seventy-second and Broadway. They have the best hot dogs in the world. Hot dogs are carcinogenic—that means they give you cancer—but so is pretty much everything else."

"Lovely," I said. "You must be a lot of fun at a cookout."

Pooch got up and went to get a fresh piece of

sandpaper out of the package I'd brought with me. He folded it in half and started rubbing it back and forth along the edge of the boat.

"If reincarnation were real," he said, "it sure would explain a lot."

I groaned. It was my own fault for having asked about what had happened to the mouse in the mousetrap, but it was clear that if I didn't stay on top of Pooch, one way or another he was going to find a way to circle back around to his favorite subject—death. And I didn't want to think about death. I'd had a dream the night my father told me about what Mike Colter had done to get himself thrown in jail. I saw Mike put his hands on the man's shoulders and push him. The dream was so vivid that when I woke up I could still hear the sound of the bones in the man's neck breaking. I'd been afraid to go back to sleep.

"We made a deal about this death stuff yesterday, remember?" I told Pooch.

"Reincarnation isn't about death," said Pooch. "It's about life. Don't you think it would be cool to get to live life all over again as something other than what you were the first time around?"

"Like what, a rock?" I said.

"Well, not a rock. That would be pretty boring.

But how about a bird?"

"I wouldn't want to be a bird, " I said. "They don't have hands. The only way they can pick anything up is with their beaks."

"I never thought about that," said Pooch. "It would be a drag not to have hands." He reached around to scratch the back of his neck. "Especially if you were itchy."

"I wouldn't mind being a horse, I guess," I said. "I think they're beautiful."

"I hate to break it to you, but horses don't have hands either," Pooch pointed out. "You don't have to come back as an animal though, you know. You could be a person. I read about this woman who swears she was Abraham Lincoln in another life."

"Do you believe that?" I asked.

"I'm not sure what I believe anymore. It all kind of changed after I met you."

Part of me wanted to come clean and tell Pooch the truth. It wasn't right for me to be making him question what he believed. Selfishly, though, I didn't want the game to end. In a way, it was almost as if the wish I'd made when I'd blown out the candles on my birthday cake had come true. I was a different person when I was with Pooch. Sure, I was Tracy

Allen's ghost, but I was also myself—my old self—the one I'd been before everything had gone wrong. All this time I'd thought it was only Annie I missed, but what I realized now was that the person I'd been missing most was me.

CHAPTER FIFTEEN

The Girl Next Door

"Why did you come looking for me anyway?" I asked Pooch later that afternoon down by the lake. "Aren't you afraid of ghosts?"

"I'm only afraid of bees," said Pooch. "And walnuts."

"Don't forget about Dixie," I added, baring my teeth and pretending to snap at him.

Pooch laughed. He had stopped sanding again and was leaning against the boat.

"Who told you to take a coffee break?" I said.

"Nobody, but don't you think maybe it's smooth enough? We've been working on it forever and there's no more sandpaper left. I took the last piece a while ago, and now it's all used up too."

My arms ached and my fingers were scraped and sore. I was just as tired of sanding as Pooch was.

"I wish we could put it in the water now," said Pooch. "Maybe the patch dried faster than we thought it would. Let's check it."

But a quick examination of the patch revealed that the boat was not ready to be launched yet.

"We're not finished anyway," I said. "We still haven't come up with a name. If we work hard on our lists tonight, maybe we'll have something by tomorrow."

"Yeah," said Pooch, "tomorrow."

As we began to gather up the tools and the crumpled pieces of used-up sandpaper, Jack, who'd been napping on a patch of moss under a tree the whole time, struggled to his feet, yawned, and stretched and looked at me expectantly.

"He sure does act like he's your dog," said Pooch.

"That doesn't mean he is," I said.

"Listen," Pooch said, "I know you're probably going to say no, but since it's still early and we can't do anything more on the boat today, do you want to maybe come over?"

I had the same problem with this idea as I'd had the day before. As curious as I was about what the inside of the Allen house might be like, I didn't want to meet Pooch's mother in my nightgown. After I'd spent two days in it working on the boat, it was not only tattered now, but also covered with dirt and pine sap. Suddenly my mother's words came floating into my head, offering me a solution.

You be me.

"Tell you what," I told Pooch. "I'll meet you at your house in half an hour."

"Honest?" said Pooch.

"Honest," I told him. "But don't be surprised if I look a little different when I show up, okay? Now turn around and cover your eyes."

It was the last time I would leave Pooch counting by the lake.

When I got home, there was a pot of spaghetti sauce simmering on the stove and my mother was in the den working on a scrapbook. She glanced at my filthy nightgown but, to my surprise, said nothing about it. I wondered if she was still mad at me for the mean thing I'd said earlier.

"It smells good in here," I told her.

"I made meatballs," she said. "You still like meatballs?"

"Of course I still like meatballs," I said.

She smiled and I smiled back at her, grateful that she didn't seem to be holding a grudge.

There was a pan of brownies cooling on the counter

out in the kitchen. *Perfect!* I thought when I saw them.

"Can I have some brownies?" I called to my mother.

"How about a sandwich first?" she called back.

I went and stood in the doorway of the den.

"They're not for me," I explained. "I was thinking about taking some brownies over to those new neighbors you were telling me about. You know, to welcome them to the neighborhood."

My mother put aside her scrapbook and stood up. She was wearing a pair of black slacks and a white blouse I didn't recognize. I wondered if her new outfit had anything to do with the comment I'd made the other day about her dress looking like a tent.

"What a nice idea," she said. "Do you want me to come along?"

"No," I said quickly, "I'd rather go alone if you don't mind."

She hesitated for a minute.

"Please don't bite my head off for asking this, Verbie, but are you going to change first? Forgive me, but that nightie looks even worse now than it did this morning."

"Don't worry," I said, "I'm going to change."

My mother's face flooded with relief.

"I'll cut you some brownies right away," she said.

Upstairs I put on a pair of shorts and a T-shirt. Then I stood in front of the mirror combing the tangles out of my hair. When I had finished, I pulled it back into a tight ponytail and fastened it with a rubber band.

"I remember you," I whispered as I tucked a loose strand of hair behind my ear.

Downstairs my mother was happily bustling around the kitchen. She had cut the brownies into squares, and she'd made me a peanut butter and grape jelly sandwich too, which I wolfed down in a couple of bites, much to her delight. Five minutes later I was standing on the porch of the Allen house knocking on the front door.

"I'm your next-door neighbor, Verbena Colter," I said when Pooch's mother came to the door. "I brought you some brownies to say welcome to the neighborhood."

Her face looked a little puffy, and you could tell that she had tried to cover the bruises under her eyes with makeup. She was wearing another tight black outfit, but instead of the fancy shoes, she had on flip-flops with little rhinestones glued on them.

I handed her the plate of brownies. She seemed surprised, but not as surprised as Pooch, who was standing behind her with his eyes popping out.

"Come in—*Verbena*, did you say?" said Pooch's mom. "Let me introduce you to my son. Shake hands with Verbena, Pooch." Dixie came running in to check me out, growling and baring her sharp little teeth at me. "Don't mind Dixie. The only one she ever actually bites is Pooch."

"I swear I didn't recognize you at first," Pooch whispered the minute we were alone. "And how'd you come up with that name?"

"It's real," I told him, "Her family lives next door. I floated over there and borrowed some of her clothes. And some brownies. And her name."

"Awesome," said Pooch.

Pooch's mom came back into the room.

"I was just about to make lunch, Verbena. Can I interest you in some tuna fish?" she asked.

"Verbena only eats marshmallows," Pooch told his mom. "And mashed potatoes."

I gave Pooch a look. He was going to have to be a lot slicker than that if this was going to work out.

"Thank you, ma'am, but I ate lunch already," I said.

132

Pooch's mother grimaced.

"*Ma'am?* That makes me sound so ancient. I'm Shari. Shari with an i." She made a little dot in the air with her finger. "I know it's a little late for lunch, but better late than never, right? Run along, you two, and I'll call you when the sandwiches are ready."

Pooch turned to me.

"Do you want to look around?" he asked.

"Sure," I said.

The house didn't have much furniture in it, and what was there was old and worn. I wondered if the Allens had taken everything with them, or if these were the same couches and chairs that Tracy and her family had sat on.

"Is it like you remember it?" asked Pooch. He sniffled. His nose was dripping, and I noticed his eyes looked a little pink.

"Not really," I said, amazed that I was actually standing inside the Allen house. Annie would never have believed it. She and I had peeked in the windows hundreds of times, fascinated by the spooky-looking shapes of the sheet-draped furniture. I had been right about the musty smell and the feeling of sadness in the air. It was hard to imagine anyone ever laughing or being happy under that roof.

Pooch sniffled again, then sneezed three times in rapid succession.

"Take your pill!" Pooch's mom called from the kitchen.

"I did!" he called back. Then he pulled a pack of tissues from his pocket, took one out, and blew his nose. "Dust," he explained, waving his hand in the air. "It's everywhere. Do you want to go upstairs now and see your room?"

I did want to see the room, but for the first time since I'd walked in the door, I felt scared. I didn't believe in ghosts. At least I didn't think I did. But after all the conversations I'd been having lately about death and reincarnation and all the rest of it, I realized I hadn't made up my mind yet what I believed.

"Are you okay?" Pooch asked. "You look kind of funny."

"I'm fine," I said. "Let's go upstairs."

Tracy Allen's old room was at the top of the stairs. There were rosebuds on the yellowed wallpaper, which was peeling in places. I walked over to the window and ran my fingers along the sill, feeling the sharp ridges in the paint where she had carved her initials. T.A. I wondered what kind of girl she'd been. Whether she'd had a best friend, or a dog who liked to follow her around. And as much as I didn't want to think about it, I couldn't help but wonder what her last moments on earth had been like too.

"Pooch!" called his mom from the foot of the stairs. *"Lunch!"*

I didn't stay while Pooch ate his lunch. I really didn't like being inside that house. I hoped that it had been a happier place when Tracy Allen had lived there and that wherever she was now she wasn't too scared or lonely.

"I'll see you in the morning," Pooch said when he took me to the door. "For the big launch, right? Do you want me to bring the rope? I think I saw some down in the basement."

"We won't need much," I told him. "I don't want to go out too deep because—"

"I know," said Pooch. "Wrinkles."

"Ten o'clock," I told him. "And remember to make your list of names tonight."

"Are you absolutely sure you don't like Tofu?" he asked.

"Positive," I told him.

* * *

Jack was sitting at the bottom of the Allens' driveway waiting for me. He'd followed me up the road as far as the house, but clearly the memory of the stone Pooch's mother had thrown at him had not faded. I was in a strange mood. It was almost as if the sad feeling inside the Allen house had rubbed off on me and a gloomy cloud was hanging over my head.

"Come on, Jackie," I said. "Let's get out of here."

When I got home, my mother was out in the yard watering her rosebushes. She had changed into her gardening clothes: a pink terry-cloth sweat suit, polka-dotted gardening gloves I'd given her for Mother's Day, and a pair of bright green rubber clogs. I thought about Pooch's mom in her tight black clothes with her fixed-up face and wondered what she would make of my mother. Honey was stretched out in a sunny spot nearby, dozing next to a cardboard box, which I assumed held the unfortunate bunnies my mother had agreed to foster. I'd hoped maybe she would be off on errands when I got back so that I would be able to be alone with my feelings for a while without being bombarded by a million questions about the visit to the new neighbors, but as soon as she saw me, my mother turned off the hose.

"How was it?" she asked, holding the nozzle away so that the hose wouldn't drip on her feet. "What were they like? Did they enjoy the brownies?"

But I couldn't answer her questions. I was too busy staring at the pile of white rags sitting on the grass at her feet. I knew right away what it was.

"What did you do?" I cried. *"What did you do?"*

CHAPTER SIXTEEN

Rain, Rain

"That nightgown had seen better days," my mother said when she saw the horrified look on my face, "so I washed it and tore it up into strips to make some bedding for the bunny. There's only one left now—the other one didn't make it. Poor thing."

I'd left my tattered nightgown on the floor of my room that afternoon when I'd changed into my clothes to go over to the Allen house. I had planned to wash it out myself and wear it again when I went to meet Pooch in the morning, but my mother had gotten to it first.

"How could you do that?" I shouted. "How could you tear it up like that without even asking?"

"You've got plenty of others in your drawer," she said, "or we can buy you a new one. I had no idea you'd react this way. Was there something special about this nightie that I didn't know?"

"It was mine."

I was upset, but my words weren't coming from the same place as the ugly thing I'd said to my mother earlier that day. This feeling was different, more like the one I'd had over at the Allen house—sad and hopeless and empty. I felt like nothing belonged to me anymore and it never would.

Dinner was a gloomy, silent affair. We sat around the kitchen table, pushing spaghetti and meatballs around our plates. My father tried to make small talk about his day at work, but eventually he gave up, and the room grew still except for the clinking of silverware and the ticking of the teapot clock hanging over the stove.

"These brownies taste different, Ellen, not like the ones you usually make," my father said when dessert was served.

"It's a new recipe," she told him. "Half regular and half nut flour. I saw it in a magazine."

"Not bad," my father said, reaching for another.

Later my mother came into my room to say good night, but I pretended that I was already asleep. I didn't want to hear her apologize again. She didn't understand that

139

it wasn't the nightgown I was upset about. After she left, I fell asleep—still in my clothes, on top of the covers—only to awaken hours later to find the house completely dark and the sound of a gentle rain falling outside. Too upset to eat at dinner, I was hungry now, so I tiptoed past my parents' bedroom and down the stairs to the kitchen for a snack of cold spaghetti and meatballs, which I ate standing up by the light of the open refrigerator door. When I had finished, I crept back upstairs and climbed under the covers. Funny, I thought, to spend two days in a nightgown and then go to bed wearing your clothes. I lay in the dark for a long time thinking, and when I finally drifted off, I had another dream, even more vivid than the last one. It was about Pooch this time. There was something really important I needed to tell him, but I couldn't seem to get him to listen to me—he kept laughing and running away. Finally I got really mad at him and started yelling, but then he lifted up his hair to show me that the reason he couldn't hear me was because he didn't have any ears.

In the morning I drifted in and out of consciousness, vaguely aware of the sound of my father's truck starting up and, later, my mother's car crunching down the gravel driveway, heading into town to help set up for the Fourth of July festivities. I looked over at the clock and sat bolt upright in bed. It was almost noon! I had promised to meet Pooch at ten. Jumping out of bed, I ran to the window. It was pouring outside. Would Pooch have gone down to the lake in this weather? Could he be down there now waiting for me? I tore off my clothes, grabbed a clean nightgown out of the drawer, and pulled it on over my head. Then I raced down the stairs, nearly tripping over Jack, who was lying on the floor pressed up against the open front door like a doorstop. He scrambled awkwardly to his feet, wagging his tail as I flew past him, but I told him "no" when he tried to follow me out of the house. I let the screen door slam shut right in his face.

Ten minutes later, soaked to the bone, I was standing breathless at the edge of Bonners Lake, but Pooch was nowhere in sight.

Along the way, my nightgown had caught in the prickers and torn, just as the other one had. Pooch might not even notice the difference. It was sticking to me like a second skin, and goose bumps the size of tapioca pearls covered my arms. I had just finished telling myself that I must have been crazy to think Pooch would come out in this kind of weather to meet me when I saw a flash of yellow moving through the trees. A minute later he stepped out of the woods, clutching the handle of a flimsy little yellow fold-up umbrella, a hunk of white nylon rope coiled over one bony shoulder.

"Did you check the patch?" he asked, coming over to stand beside me so that I could get under the umbrella with him. "Is it ruined?"

The umbrella was too small to protect us both from the rain.

"I just got here," I said, putting my hand over his on the umbrella handle to steady it.

"Oh good," he said, relieved. "I wasn't sure if I should come earlier or not, but then I remembered what you'd said about getting wet." He looked at my night-gown. "You do look kind of wrinkled."

A drop of rainwater slid down Pooch's nose. He scrunched up his face, wiggling his nose like a rabbit to shake it free. I suddenly flashed on my dream from the night before. The bunnies. That must have been why I'd dreamed that Pooch had no ears. Dreams have such a funny way of sifting out random pieces and stitching them together like a crazy quilt.

"Guess there aren't going to be any fireworks tonight, huh?" said Pooch disappointedly.

"You can still go to the band concert—they always

play no matter what," I told him.

"Really?" he said.

The rain began to slow, and when the sky suddenly cleared, Pooch folded up the little yellow umbrella and jammed it into one of his many pockets. Together we walked over to the boat to check on the patch.

"It seems tight," he said, running his hands over the piece of pale bark. "Let's tip it over and dump the rainwater out."

Together we tipped the boat, and as we rocked it back into place again the sun came out. Grateful for the warmth, I hoped it would stay out long enough to dry my nightgown.

"Did you bring your list?" asked Pooch.

In my haste to get down to the lake, I'd left the list of boat names behind on the little night table beside my bed. I'd been too upset the night before to put more thought into it anyway.

"They weren't very good," I told Pooch.

"Mine either," he said. "Maybe we need to get in and float around for a while for inspiration."

I looked at him skeptically.

"Okay, maybe I just want to see if it floats—don't you?" he asked.

"Give me one end of that rope," I told him. "I'll tie it to the boat, and you go tie the other end to that tree over there."

"Cool," said Pooch.

In all the times I'd been down to Bonners Lake, I had never so much as stuck a toe in the water, but in order to launch the boat, it was necessary for us both to wade out into the lake. As the chilly water rose first above my ankles, and then up to my knees, I shivered. It was hard not to think about how deep it might be out in the middle. I could have made up some kind of an excuse to keep from having to go out in the boat with Pooch. He would have believed anything I told him. But as long as the rope was tied tight and was only long enough to let us out a little ways, I thought I could handle it. I had worked as hard as Pooch getting the boat ready; I wanted to share in the glory of the launch.

As soon as the boat was free of the mud, Pooch, who had taken off his shoes and socks and rolled up the legs of his pants, threw a leg over the side and scrambled in.

"It's awesome!" he cried.

"Is the patch holding?" I asked.

Pooch leaned down and put his hand on the spot

where the hole had been.

"Dry as a bone," he announced with a grin. "Come on. Get in."

I glanced nervously back at the tree where Pooch had tied the rope before we pushed the boat out.

"Did you double knot it?" I asked.

"Don't worry," said Pooch. "I know about knots. I read a whole book about them. I'm practically an expert."

Climbing into a boat in a nightgown while trying to maintain your dignity is no easy feat. My arms were too weak to hoist myself over the side, so Pooch had to take my hands and pull me in. In the process I did a lot of kicking and thrashing around, gathering a number of painful splinters in some very tender spots. The boat definitely could have used a bit more sanding. When I finally managed to get in, I was soaking wet again and we were both out of breath. Pooch sat down on the middle seat, and I was crawling along the bottom of the boat to sit in the back when I noticed that we were drifting.

CHAPTER SEVENTEEN

Hello Trouble

Pooch quickly scrambled up to the bow of the boat and pulled on the rope, but there was no tension—it was limp in his hands. The knot on the other end had come untied.

"I used a granny knot," Pooch said. "I've made it a million times. You pass the right end over and under the left. Or wait, maybe it's the other way around."

"*You idiot!*" I screamed.

"I'm sorry," he said.

"Sorry doesn't help. Get out quick and pull us back in before we drift any farther."

A miserable look came over Pooch's face.

"I can't," he said.

"*Why not?*"

"I can't swim." He peered over the side of the boat. "And I don't see the bottom anymore."

Since we didn't have oars, the plan had been to pull ourselves, hand over hand, back to shore with the rope when we were done. We tried leaning over the sides and paddling like mad, but our arms were too short, and it got us nowhere.

For a minute we sat, stunned, drifting in silence.

"Wait a second!" said Pooch, smacking his forehead with the heel of his hand. "I just thought of something. *You're a ghost!* You can fly! You can pull us in with the rope and you won't even have to get wet. Or we could ask some of the other ghosts you know to come and help us."

I did not want to have to tell Pooch that he'd been duped by a girl in a ripped-up nightgown, who could neither fly nor summon ghosts, but clearly the time had come to tell the truth.

At first he didn't believe me.

"Come on," he said, "quit fooling."

"No, really," I told him. "I'm not a ghost. I never even met Tracy Allen. My name is Verbena Colter and I live in that big white house next door to where you and your mom are staying. And I hate to tell you this, but I can't swim either."

When Pooch realized I wasn't kidding, he was devastated.

"You lied to me?" he said, his face crumpled in disbelief. *"About everything?"*

"Well you lied to me too about being able to tie a knot," I said defensively. "If you'd done it right, we wouldn't be in this mess."

"I thought you were my friend," he said.

It would have been easier if he'd gotten mad, yelled at me, and called me names. But he was hurt and as terrified as I was to be drifting untethered in that boat, I felt even worse about what I'd done to Pooch. I'd known from the beginning that it was wrong, and I'd gone ahead and done it anyway. Not only that, but I'd enjoyed it, both the pretending part and the sense of power it had given me over him. I didn't see any point in trying to explain that I couldn't help being the way I was. Why should he care? I was the one who had to live with myself.

"I'm sorry," I told him.

"Yeah, well sorry doesn't help, remember?"

He turned his back to me, and I could tell from the way his shoulders were shaking that he was crying. I didn't know what to do, so I just waited. After a while he stopped and wiped his nose on his sleeve.

"What are we going to do now?" he asked me,

without turning around.

"Are you sure you don't know how to swim?"

"I'm sure," he said.

"Did you tell your mom you were coming here?"

Pooch shook his head.

Of course my parents didn't know where I was either, and with all the Fourth of July preparations going on in town, there was no telling when they might come home.

We had drifted about fifteen feet from shore by then. It seemed so close and yet impossibly far away. Pooch started scratching. If I looked at the water, I felt sick, but I discovered that if I looked up at the sky, I could fool myself into thinking we weren't out that far.

"Maybe if we yell for help, someone will hear us," I said.

I started yelling, and pretty soon Pooch joined in. After ten minutes of shouting at the top of our lungs, the only response we got was the mocking metallic screech of a pair of blue jays scolding us from the top of a tree.

"Now what?" said Pooch.

The wind was beginning to pick up a little, which gave me an idea.

"Maybe we could make a sail out of something," I suggested.

"How about your nightgown?"

"Uh, I don't think so," I said, wrapping my arms around myself with a shiver. "How about the umbrella?"

Pooch knelt on the seat at the bow of the boat, opened the little yellow umbrella, and held it out in front of him, but nothing happened.

Bonners Lake was not nearly as big as an ocean, but as lakes went, it was a pretty big one. There were no houses around it, and trees and thick brush grew right up to the edges and, in places, right out into the water. The main body of the lake, where Pooch and I were floating, was rounded at one end and split off into two arms down at the other. Once you entered either of those arms, you would no longer be visible from the end of the lake where we'd started.

"Do you think we should try yelling some more?" I asked Pooch.

"Nobody heard us the last time."

"I think we should do it anyway, just in case," I said.

So we yelled again for help, but this time even the blue jays didn't respond.

Pooch had moved back to the middle seat and was

scratching and wriggling around nervously.

"You okay?" I asked.

"Not really," he said. "I need to go."

"Someone will come looking for us eventually," I said. "If I'm not home by dark, my parents will send out a search party for sure."

"That's not what I meant," said Pooch, "I have to *go*."

"Oh," I said.

"What should I do?"

"Can't you hold it in?" I asked him.

"I've been doing that for a while," he said, "but now I've really got to go."

There was nothing in the boat that he could use, so I suggested the only thing I could think of.

"Do it over the side."

"No way," said Pooch.

"Okay, then you'll have to hold it 'til somebody comes and pulls us back in."

We sat for a few minutes. The wind, stronger now, made the water choppy, so it slapped against the side of the boat. Pooch wriggled uncomfortably.

"If I do it over the side, do you promise you won't look?" he asked finally.

"Don't worry," I told him. "I don't want to see."

He squinched up his eyebrows and gave me a good

hard look. I knew he must be wondering why in the world he should trust me after what I'd done.

"I'm not going to look, Pooch," I told him. "Cross my heart and hope to die." I drew a little X on my nightie with my finger the way he had always done with me. Then I turned around and covered my eyes.

When he was finished, Pooch sat back down.

"Thanks," he said.

The likelihood of someone coming down to fish in the middle of the day wasn't very high, and half an hour later, when the sky grew dark and the rain started up again, our chances of being discovered by accident diminished further. Pooch raised the yellow umbrella, and I was grateful when he invited me to move up to the middle seat to sit beside him. At first he was stiff, holding himself upright so that our bodies wouldn't touch at all, but the rain was cold and the umbrella small, and pretty soon he relaxed and allowed himself to lean against me. When he started to sniffle again, I put my arm around him.

"Don't worry, Pooch," I said. "Someone's going to come. We just have to wait."

I had no idea how long we'd been out there. Neither of us was wearing a watch, and it was hard to tell what time of day it was because the sky was so dark. It rained off and on, and although the sun peeked out every now and then, it was never out long enough to dry our clothes all the way through. The boat continued to drift, and when we were about twenty-five feet from shore, it stopped and began turning in a lazy circle, caught up in a current of some kind.

Pressed up against him, I could feel Pooch shaking, or maybe it was both of us. It was hard to look up at the sky from underneath the umbrella, so I closed my eyes to keep from having to see the water. There was something nagging at me, something I needed to do. I didn't want to alarm Pooch, but neither of us had checked on the patch to see if it was still holding.

CHAPTER EIGHTEEN

Tick Tock

Pooch was scratching again, and when I opened my eyes to look at him, I could see that there were angry red hives staining the backs of his hands. Checking on the patch would have to wait—he was upset enough as it was.

I thought about my mother and wondered what she would do if she were in my place. I remembered a trick she'd used to distract me when I'd been little and scared about having to get a shot at the doctor.

"Let's sing," I said in a chipper voice that mimicked the one she'd always used with me.

"*Sing?*" said Pooch.

"To make the time pass more quickly."

"I can't carry a tune," he said.

"That doesn't matter," I told him. "Nobody's listening but me. Do you know 'Miss Mary Mack'? I'll teach you how the clapping part goes too. Put down the umbrella—you'll need both hands."

It wasn't raining anymore, so Pooch put down the umbrella and I taught him the words to the song.

Miss Mary Mack Mack Mack
All dressed in black, black, black
With silver buttons, buttons, buttons
All down her back, back, back.

She asked her mother, mother, mother
For fifty cents, cents, cents
To see the elephants, elephants, elephants
Jump over the fence, fence, fence.

They jumped so high, high, high
They reached the sky, sky, sky
And they didn't come back, back, back
'Til the Fourth of July, ly, ly.

Pooch made a halfhearted attempt to learn the clapping game that went along with the words, but his eyes kept darting around nervously, and the hives had spread to his neck and cheeks now.

"What if nobody comes?" he asked, rubbing the backs of his itchy hands down the legs of his pants to scratch them. "What if we have to sit out here all night? What if there's a tornado and we tip over? Or a giant wave fills the boat with water and we sink?"

I had to think of something fast to stop Pooch's growing list of terrible what-ifs before he drove us both over the edge into full-blown panic. I didn't know enough about dinosaurs to carry on an intelligent conversation, and although I knew he was fascinated with the subject of ghosts and death, under the circumstances I didn't think it was a good time to bring that up. So I took a chance and guessed at another topic that I thought Pooch might want to talk about.

"Tell me about New York City."

People in Clydesdale called New York City "The Dirty Side," but everybody I'd ever met who lived there thought that it was something special. Pooch perked up immediately when I asked him about it.

"Have you ever been?" he said.

"Actually, I was born there," I told him, and when he looked at me as if he didn't believe me, I added, "At Mount Sinai Hospital."

Apparently that little detail was enough to convince him.

"No way!" he cried excitedly. "That's where I was

born too! I almost died because I came two months early. They had to stick a lot of tubes in me so I could breathe."

"I almost died too," I told him.

"Really? How come?"

It wasn't the direction I had thought the conversation would go in, but after all the lies I had told Pooch, I thought maybe telling him the truth for a change might undo some of the damage.

"My real mom was an alcoholic. She's the reason I look the way I do. And I got my mean streak from my real dad. He's in jail for killing someone."

Pooch didn't say anything, so I figured maybe I'd gone too far and he was back to thinking that I was lying to him, but then I noticed that he was looking past me toward shore.

"Look!" he said, pointing.

Someone had heard our cries for help after all.

"Jack!"

As soon as he heard his name, Jack began running back and forth along the edge of the water barking frantically.

"He's a good swimmer, right?" Pooch said. "If we get him to come out to us, we can tie the rope to his collar and he can pull us back in."

I crooked my pinkie and whistled.

"Come on, boy!" I called, clapping my hands. "Come and get us, Jackie boy."

It didn't take much coaxing to get Jack into the water. Soon only his head and the tip of his tail were visible as he paddled steadily toward us. He was a strong swimmer despite his missing leg, and in no time at all he had reached the boat. Pooch scrambled up to the front and quickly began to pull in the rope. When the soggy frayed end finally floated into sight, he fished it out and handed it to me so I could lean over the side and attach it to Jack's collar.

"Careful!" warned Pooch as we tipped and the edge of the boat came precariously close to the water.

I told Pooch to scoot over and sit up on the opposite side of the boat to balance us while I tried once more to lean out and tie the rope to Jack's collar.

"Every time I get close, he swims away again," I said.

I made several more attempts, but each time I reached for him, Jack would swim away. After a while he stopped coming near the boat at all and began paddling a few feet away in a big circle around us.

"What's he doing?" asked Pooch.

"I think he's protecting us."

We sat in the boat watching as Jack continued to circle, his big paws paddling in a steady rhythm, head tipped back and ears floating out to the sides like wings. It started to rain again, but we didn't bother to put up the umbrella.

"Dumb dog," I muttered in frustration.

"We could write a note and stick it under his collar," suggested Pooch.

"We don't have anything to write on, and a note would just disintegrate when it got wet anyway. The rope is the best idea—we just have to figure out a way to get him to come closer."

"Hey," said Pooch suddenly, "does Jack like chocolate?"

"He's not allowed to eat chocolate. Why? Do you have some?"

Pooch started patting the pockets of his pants.

"I just remembered," he said. "I've got one of those brownies you brought over yesterday. I never got a chance to taste them, so I stuck one in here somewhere in case I got hungry later and needed a snack." He finally found the right pocket, reached in, and pulled out a neat little square of tinfoil. "We can use it to bribe Jack. I won't feed it to him. I'll just let him sniff it—then while he's distracted, you can put the rope around his neck."

It was worth a try. Pooch unwrapped the brownie, got down on his knees, and held it over the side of the boat for Jack.

"Come and get it, boy," he called. "Nice yummy brownie, just for you."

Jack slowed down long enough to sniff the air but decided he wasn't interested and kept swimming.

"Too bad you don't have any cat food in your pockets," I said. "I know he likes that."

Finally Pooch gave up and sat back down in the boat, defeated. He looked at the brownie in his hand. Then he held it up to his face and studied it closely.

"I don't see any nuts in this, do you?" he asked.

I glanced at the brownie and shrugged. I was trying to think if there was any other way to get Jack to come closer.

"What about if we made a loop and tried to toss it over his head as he swims by?" I asked.

"Like Sugarfoot, you mean?"

"Who's Sugarfoot?" I asked.

"Some cowboy my dad used to watch on TV when he was little." Pooch held the brownie out to me. "Want half?"

I shook my head. Pooch bit off a corner of the brownie and began to chew while I turned my attention back to Jack, who was still circling the boat.

"Hand me the rope and let's see if I can make a loop," I said.

Pooch didn't answer.

"Hurry up, hand me the rope," I said again. "Here he comes."

Pooch coughed, and when I looked over at him, his face was bright red and he had his hand on his throat.

"What's wrong?" I asked, alarmed. "Are you choking?"

He shook his head. His eyes were bulging.

"Nuts," he gasped, letting what was left of the brownie slip out of his hand and fall into the bottom of the boat. *"There must be nuts."*

CHAPTER NINETEEN

No, No, No

Pooch was wheezing and clawing at his face with his fingernails. When he opened his mouth, I could see that his tongue was horribly swollen. He closed his eyes and slid off the seat into the bottom of the boat, and he lay there shaking while panic rose inside me in hot waves. My mother had made those brownies and only now, now when it was too late, did I remember what she'd said about the recipe. *Half regular flour, half nut flour.* The nut flour must have been made from walnuts! What was it he'd told me about his allergy attacks? There was something, but I couldn't think straight, I was so terrified.

"Tell me what to do, Pooch," I said. "I don't know how to help you."

But Pooch didn't answer; his whole body was shaking so violently now, it rocked the boat.

"Help!" I screamed at the top of my lungs. "Somebody, help!"

I don't remember getting into the water, I only remember that it was cold. I must have scraped my face as I went over the side, because my cheek stung, and somehow I managed to knock my glasses off and lose them. Clinging to the side with both hands, and blind as a bat, I began to inch my way toward the back of the boat.

"Please don't die, Pooch," I whispered. "Please don't die."

My nightgown floated up around me like a cloud in a bottle green sky. When I reached the back of the boat, I hung there by my arms for a minute, stunned and shivering, and then I began to kick my feet the way I'd learned to do with a kickboard in the Washerville swimming pool. After a while I looked to the side, and to my great relief I could make out the jagged blur of trees changing shape as we slowly slipped past. It was working. We were moving toward shore.

Jack came and swam next to me, close enough that his big paws grazed my side underwater as he paddled. Now that he was within easy reach, I could have tried to tie the rope to him again, but it might not have worked and there wasn't any time to spare. There was no sound coming from inside the boat; Pooch wasn't moving at all anymore.

I was out of breath and completely numb when I finally touched bottom with my feet. I quickly pulled the boat up onto shore and climbed in. Pooch was lying still in the bottom of the boat and didn't answer or open his eyes even when I shook him. Fearing the worst, I laid my head on his chest—and burst into grateful tears when I felt it rise and fall. Maybe it was the flood of relief that unclouded my brain long enough for my memory to retrieve the word—*EpiPen!*

Frantically I searched Pooch's pockets, yanking out soggy tissue packs and several stashes of his little glass bottles until finally I found what I was looking for. Luckily the instructions were printed on the side of the EpiPen, and although I was as good as blind without my glasses, I was able to read them by holding the package up close to my face. I did what it said to do: pressed the black tip of the tube into the side of Pooch's thigh and held it there while I counted to five. Then I dropped the EpiPen on the ground beside the boat and ran to get help.

I never would have made it home without Jack. He was my eyes, leading me along the path. When I finally stumbled out of the woods, I ran across the yard and up the front steps crying, *"Come quick! Come quick!"* but the house was completely dark and there was nobody home to hear my cries. Even without my glasses on I could tell that there was something odd about the way the door looked. When I ran my hands over it searching for the handle, I discovered that it was broken, hanging cock-eyed from one hinge, a large hole in the mesh where Jack had pushed through the screen to get out. I tried to pull it open, but it was jammed, so I stood dripping wet on the porch, trying to figure out what to do next. The sound of my pounding heart echoed in my ears until it slowly dawned on me that the hollow steady thumping was not my heart at all, but the bass drum of the Clydesdale Band beating in the distance.

Annie and I had ridden our bikes down the hill into town many times together. Once she had even dared me to do it with my eyes closed. I thought about that time as I sped along on my bike through the dusky light, the blur of the dirt road flying by beneath me with only the sound of the band to guide me into town. I had left Jack at home, locked in the garage, whining. I was afraid that if I let him come along, he might run too close to the bike and accidentally knock me off or hurt himself. The music grew louder the closer I got, and finally I skidded around the corner onto Main Street, where I could make out the shape of the crowd gathered in front of the bandstand. I got off my bike, letting it fall with a clatter to the ground. I can only imagine how I must have looked in my tattered nightgown, pushing through the crowd and jumping up onto the bandstand, wild-eyed and screaming for my mother. She was the only one I wanted and, like Honey, I had found my way to her.

"What is it, Verbena?" my mother said, as I clung to her, sobbing uncontrollably in front of the stunned crowd. "What's happened?"

The next part is a jumble. My father and some other local men left immediately to get Pooch. Because there was no road down to Bonners Lake, they had to go on foot. We didn't know the phone number over at the Allen house, so my mother and I went and got Pooch's mom and told her what had happened. By the time they carried Pooch out of the woods, it was dark out and the ambulance was waiting for him in our driveway.

I remember how cold the speckled rock felt under my bare muddy feet that night as I stood on it, watching the flashing red lights of the ambulance disappear down the hill into the darkness. My mother came and stood beside me.

"It's all my fault," I told her. "I knew about the nut flour. I just forgot. I'll never forgive myself if—"

"It's not in your hands," my mother said, putting her arm around me. "Come inside now and we'll find you something dry to put on."

My mother tried to comfort me, but I couldn't stop thinking about how Pooch looked, lying there so small and helpless on the stretcher as they lifted him into the ambulance. Pooch had told me he believed death was a natural part of living. But I didn't want to live in a world that could take someone as good as Pooch away forever, while someone as rotten as me got a second chance.

"It's not fair," I sobbed. "We have to do something."

"All we can do now is pray," my mother told me.

It was midnight when my father called to tell us that Pooch was out of danger. The doctors decided to keep him overnight for observation just to be sure, but he was going to be fine. I had been far too upset to eat or sleep, but after my father's phone call, I ate two bowls of chicken noodle soup, then curled up on the couch under a blanket with my head in my mother's lap. Honey came and sat on the arm of the couch, and Jack, exhausted, lay snoring on the floor beside me. He was still damp from being in the lake and he smelled awful, but I didn't care.

I reached down and worked my fingers into his fur, and I fell asleep with my hand resting on his back.

The next morning my mother dug up an old pair of glasses for me to wear until we could have some new ones made. She brought me cinnamon toast with the crusts cut off, and a cup of hot chocolate with a mountain of marshmallows floating in it.

"Do you want a bite?" I asked, holding out a piece of toast to her.

She looked at it. "I shouldn't," she said, shaking her head.

I felt bad. She was probably saying no because of the mean things I'd said to her about her weight.

"You look really pretty today, Mom," I told her.

She studied me, and her face softened.

"Thank you," she said. When she turned to leave, I reached for her. "Don't go," I said.

I scooched over to make room for my mother, and she came and sat beside me on the couch. There was something I needed to get off my chest.

"I know I wasn't supposed to be down at the lake," I began, "and I know that I shouldn't have lied to Pooch. You probably think I don't know right from wrong, but it isn't true."

My mother started to say something when there was a loud thump directly behind us—a sound we both knew meant that a bird had just hit the window. All the feeders hanging in the yard brought the birds in close to the house, and sometimes they would confuse a reflection in the glass for open sky. Whenever it happened, we would run outside to check. Usually the bird would have flown away already, and we'd never even know what kind it had been, but this time, when we turned to look at the window, there was an ominous spot of orange and a tiny white feather stuck to the glass.

My mother stood up and I followed her out into the yard, where we found a small bluish-gray bird lying in the grass beneath the window.

"Poor little thing," she said, bending over it. "It's just a baby."

The tiny bird was opening and closing its beak rapidly, but no sound came out.

"Should we take it to Dr. Finn?" I asked.

My mother shook her head.

"Better to leave it be," she said.

The little fledgling spread its wings and raised its tail up and down a few times, as if testing to see if all the parts were still working. For a second I felt hopeful. Maybe once it had rested for a bit, it would recover enough to fly away. But after a while the fluttering of its wings against the grass caused it to fall over onto its side, where it flopped helplessly for a minute until finally, exhausted, it lay still. The way it was tipped up, I could see its legs tucked underneath it, two brown cherry stems held tightly against its pale breast, the long delicate toes curled into tiny fists.

"Let's go back inside," my mother urged.

"No," I said, "I want to stay."

I sank down in the grass, and my mother got down beside me. It lasted only a few minutes, the bird lying still throughout, with the exception of its rapid breathing and the beak, which continued to open and close in silent song until the very end.

I had seen dead animals along the side of the road, and fish washed up on the edge of Bonners Lake, but I had never witnessed the exact moment when life passed out of a creature. It was the most terrible and at the same time the most beautiful thing I had ever seen. I started to cry, and my mother put her arm around me.

"These things happen," she said, trying to comfort me.

But it wasn't the bird I was crying about.

"Please don't send me away," I said.

"What on earth are you talking about?" she asked.

"Like Teddy," I said, "and Uncle Mike. I know I'm warped, just like them, but I can't help it. It's like some kind of poison got poured into me and it's turning me into somebody I don't want to be. I promise I'll try to do better. I do know right from wrong. Please don't give up on me."

"Oh, Verbie," my mother said, "how could you think that I would do such a thing? Send you away? You are my whole world. I couldn't live without you. Don't you know that?"

"But I'm bad," I sobbed, the words catching in my throat like the tiny claws on the ends of the little dead bird's toes.

She took my face in her hands and held it tight until I'd caught my breath.

"I want you to listen to me very carefully," she said. "You are not like Teddy or your uncle Mike. Do you hear me? You are sweet, and good, and kind."

"I lied to Pooch and he almost died."

"He's lucky to have a friend like you," my mother said.

"*Lucky?*"

"You saved his life, Verbie. You were such a brave

girl to do what you did. I've never been more proud to be your mama."

"You're just saying that to be nice. But no amount of nice can fix what's wrong with me. You said so yourself."

"There's nothing wrong with you, little girl," my mother said. "You're just growing up is all. Feeling mixed up and mad at the world is a part of that for almost everyone. It certainly was for me. I gave my parents a real run for their money—especially my mother. It'll pass, Sugarpea. I promise."

When she called me by that name, I started to cry again, even harder this time. She put her arms around me and rocked me back and forth just like Pooch and I had rocked the boat to loosen it from the mud.

"Poor little thing," she whispered, "poor little thing."

I buried my face in her neck and closed my eyes, and we sat like that for a very long time. Mama and her Sugarpea.

We put the baby bird in a cardboard box and buried it under the lilac bush. I had never been to a funeral, except for the one in the fourth-grade play, so after we had covered the box with dirt I said the only words I knew that might be appropriate.

My beloved,
As the moon grows pale and slips from the night sky,
Do not be afraid.
I will find you in the sparrow's song,
And in the firefly's light.
Do not be afraid, my beloved.
Your soul will live forever in my heart.

CHAPTER TWENTY

Heart of My Heart

My grandpa Colty died on the same day I was born, and I don't believe that was an accident. I think he knew I was going to need all the help I could get navigating what lay ahead for me. Whether or not he gave me his soul is something I may never know for sure, but that summer between fifth and sixth grade when I was trying to find myself, it gave me great comfort to know that either way, he still would have been my grandfather.

Because of the rain, the Fourth of July fireworks display was postponed until the following Saturday. That morning Pooch showed up on our doorstep bright and early.

"Good morning, Robert," my mother said when she

opened the door to let him in. "You're just in time for pancakes."

Pooch had been coming over to our house every day since he'd gotten out of the hospital. My mother absolutely adored him—except for his nickname. She didn't like the story about how he had gotten it—she thought it was mean—so she refused to call him Pooch, insisting instead on Robert.

"Do you want real maple syrup, or do you prefer the store-bought kind, Robert?" my mother called from the kitchen.

"Store-bought, please!" he called back.

"Did you remember to take your pill?" I asked him as we walked to the kitchen together.

Pooch grinned.

"You guys sure are alike," he said. "Like two peas in a pod."

My mother looked over at me and we both smiled. There were plenty of things she and I didn't see eye to eye on, but I was beginning to understand that in all the ways that really mattered, we were more alike than I had ever realized.

"Take your medicine," I told Pooch.

"Aye aye, Captain," he said.

Pooch pulled his allergy medicine out of his pocket, flipped the cap off the plastic bottle, and popped a pill into his mouth. If he forgot to take his medicine before he came over to our house, he would spend the whole time sneezing. Our house wasn't dusty, but it was full of all kinds of other things that Pooch was allergic to, including the little bunny with the missing ears.

"Where is she?" he asked, looking around.

"Where do you think?" I said, pointing to the corner.

Jack was lying curled up on the rug, with the bunny sleeping between his paws. They had become fast friends and were never far from each other. Pooch bent down and patted Jack on the head, then gently picked up the bunny.

"Who's the cutest little thing in the whole wide world?" he cooed, rubbing the soft brown fur against his cheek.

"Turn it down a notch, Pooch," I told him. "Otherwise, I'm warning you, I'm gonna be sick."

"Well she *is* the cutest thing," he said, "Look at her. Who could resist that face?"

"I feel sorry for her," I said. "We should never have let you pick out her name. She's *brown*, in case you haven't noticed."

"So what," he said, putting the bunny back down on the rug, "Tofu's a perfect name for a bunny. And you never know—she might turn white later on when she gets older."

"You don't know much about animals, do you?" I said.

After breakfast, Pooch and I went out in the yard.

"What do you want to do?" I asked.

"We could pick blackberries," he said. "Your mom said if we got enough, she'd make a pie. Your mom sure is nice."

I had been worried at first, what Pooch would make of my mother, she was so different from his mom. But they hit it off right away. In fact sometimes it seemed like he came over as much to see my mother as to see me. She thought he was "cute as a button" and he didn't mind it one bit that she liked to feed him. I don't think Shari minded that either. I was glad that Pooch and my mom got along, and I was glad she had someone else to fuss over other than me, but I have to admit, every now and then I did feel a little jealous. It's a wonderful thing, knowing that you're somebody's whole world, and I had no intention of sharing that place in my mother's heart, even with Pooch.

It was a perfect day for berry picking, sunny but not too hot.

"There's a bucket in the garage," I said to Pooch. "Come on."

The blackberries were plentiful and we laughed and joked as we moved from bush to bush working together to fill the silver bucket to the top.

"Did you know that you can die from having the hiccups for too long?" Pooch told me, tossing a berry up in the air and trying to catch it in his mouth. "I read it in a book."

"Did you know that you can die from reading too many books?" I said.

Pooch looked at me.

"Are you grumpy today?" he asked.

"I'm grumpy every day," I said, pushing up my glasses with a knuckle. "In case you haven't noticed,"

"I've noticed," said Pooch, "but I don't mind. It's part of who you are."

"Yeah," I said. "At least for now."

It took us about forty-five minutes to fill the bucket with berries. We were so busy picking and talking, neither of us realized how far we'd come until Pooch pointed through the trees at a patch of sparkling green. Bonners Lake. We hadn't been back, either one of us,

178

since the incident in the boat.

"Do you want to go take a look?" I asked him.

"Do you?"

The boat was right where we'd left it, the ground around it covered with footprints that told the whole story. In among the big waffle-soled boot prints of the men who'd come to carry Pooch out of the woods, the tracks of my small bare feet were still visible, Jack's paw prints right beside them.

"Do you care if we don't ever come back here again?" I asked Pooch. "It kind of creeps me out. You could have died, you know."

"I know."

"I'm glad you didn't die, Pooch."

"I never told you this," said Pooch, "but when I found out that you weren't really a ghost, even though I was mad, I was also really happy. I'm glad you didn't die either."

As we stood looking at the boat, it suddenly dawned on me that the shape of it reminded me of something.

"What would you think about *The Peapod* as a name?" I asked Pooch.

"*The Peapod?*"

He tilted his head to one side, considering. "Now

that you mention it, I guess it does kind of look like one. It's even got a curly rope stem at the tip. Yeah, *The Peapod* would be a good name! If only we had some paint."

"We do," I said.

Crouching down beside the bucket, I picked out a handful of the biggest, juiciest blackberries I could find, and holding them between my fingers, I used the purple juice to stain the letters onto the side of the boat.

"What do you think?" I asked Pooch when I was finished.

"Sweet," he said.

That night, after dark, Pooch and I lay next to each other on the blue blanket and watched the fireworks bursting overhead. At the end of the month when he left to go spend time with his father, it broke my heart to see him go. I got a postcard from him about a week later. It was from Fire Island and it had a picture of a boat on it. He'd scratched off the name on the stern and written SPINACH in its place. Several days later I got another postcard in the mail, this one from Annie. She was full of complaints about the awful food at camp and the bratty kids in her cabin, and how horrible and boring her whole summer had turned out to be. At the bottom of the card she had run out of space, so she'd turned it and written the end of her message going up the side. "I miss you, Verbie," it said. "Love, Annie."

That August was endlessly rainy, and the mosquitoes were so bad I spent a lot of time cooped up inside the house. My mother and I tangled plenty, but no matter how heated it got, I didn't worry anymore. I knew she wasn't going anywhere, and neither was I.

Sixth grade turned out to be a good year for me. For one thing, I grew five inches. Even better, Heather Merwin got herself a new best friend and things between Annie and me went back to normal. The lilacs bloomed in May the way they were supposed to, and on the last day of school, while Annie sat on the porch steps waiting, my mother took a picture of me standing in front of her roses with a big smile on my face. Years later I can look at that picture and still remember the way I felt as if it were only yesterday. Life is complicated sometimes to be sure, but there are other times, like that day, standing on the near edge of a new July, when life is just as sweet, and good, and simple as it seems.

Author's Note

Fetal alcohol syndrome, or FAS, is the name given to a group of physical and mental birth defects that are caused by drinking alcohol during pregnancy. Once the damage is done, it cannot be undone, but FAS is the only birth defect that can be completely prevented—by not drinking alcohol during pregnancy.